A Candlelight Ecstasy Romance ™

"YOU'RE THAT GOOD, ARE YOU?" SHE SNEERED AT HIM—AND AT HER OWN UNCERTAINTY. . . .

"I'm that good." His flat agreement, delivered without a hint of bravado, drew a shocked gasp from Jen. Before she could form the jumbled words of defensive ridicule that crowded into her mind, he added forcefully, "But my expertise—for want of a better word—has nothing to do with it. You have been mine for the taking from the moment we met. I know it, and although your mind's been dodging around in a frantic attempt to deny it, you know it too."

"Adam," Jen faltered, swallowing her outrage, "what is it you want?"

"Exactly what I'm willing to give," he answered without hesitation. "Unconditional surrender."

SNOWBOUND WEEKEND

Amii Lorin

A CANDLELIGHT ECSTASY ROMANCE™

Published by
Dell Publishing Co., Inc.
1 Dag Hammarskjold Plaza
New York, New York 10017

Dell ® TM 681510, Dell Publishing Co., Inc.

Candlelight Ecstasy Romance™ is a trademark of
Dell Publishing Co., Inc., New York, New York.

ISBN: 0-440-18027-9

Printed in the United States of America

First printing—April 1982

Dear Reader:

In response to your continued enthusiasm for Candlelight Ecstasy Romances™, we are increasing the number of new titles from four to six per month.

We are delighted to present sensuous novels set in America, depicting modern American men and women as they confront the provocative problems of modern relationships.

Throughout the history of the Candlelight line, Dell has tried to maintain a high standard of excellence to give you the finest in reading enjoyment. That is and will remain our most ardent ambition.

Anne Gisonny
Editor
Candlelight Romances

SNOWBOUND WEEKEND

CHAPTER 1

The alarm rang at four thirty. A soft groan preceded the slim pale hand that emerged from under the brightly colored paisley comforter to depress the shutoff button. Yawning sleepily, Jen followed her arm out of the warm cocoon of bedding into the chill air of the bedroom. Still partially asleep, she pushed her way out of the tangle of covers and sat up. The sudden shrill ringing of the phone on the bookcase headboard of the bed brought her fully awake with a start. *Who in the world would be calling at this hour?* Eyeing the instrument warily, she lifted the receiver, hesitated, then said crisply, "Hello?"

"Jen?"

The dry, croaking voice was hardly recognizable as belonging to her friend Chris.

"Yes, of course it's me," she answered. Then, frowning, she asked, "Why are you whispering?"

"I'm not," Chris rasped. "Oh, Jen, I can't go."

Can't go? Chris's words didn't register for a second. *Can't go!* Then they sank in with a bang.

"What do you mean you can't go?" Jen exclaimed loudly. "The trip's been paid for for weeks. The bus leaves in an hour and a half. Four thirty is a bad time of the morning for making jokes, Chris."

"I wish it was a joke," Chris wailed raggedly. "I'm sick, Jen. I've been up all night doctoring a sore throat, but it hasn't helped. My mother just took my temp and it's 101.6. She says there is no way she is going to let me go

9

off into the mountains for a weekend." Chris paused to cough roughly, then went on, "And to tell you the truth, I don't have the strength to argue with her about it. Right now all I want to do is lie down and die." Again the dry, rough-sounding cough came over the wire. "I'm sorry, Jen."

"Don't be silly," Jen scolded gently. "You didn't try to get sick." Submerging her own disappointment, she sympathized, "What rotten luck. I don't suppose there's any way you can get a refund?"

"Mother's going to call Liz in a half hour to tell her I'm sick," Chris croaked. "I did take the insurance against just such a contingency." Her voice was beginning to sound reedy, tired. "Didn't you?"

"No," Jen laughed ruefully. "Or I'd call and cancel too. The cost of the trip alone was enough, and as I hardly ever get sick, I never even considered it. But I'm glad you did."

"Oh, Jen," Chris half sighed, half coughed, "I feel terrible about this. I hope you have a good time."

Jen bit her lip at the sound of tears in her friend's voice. What was she thinking of, keeping Chris on the phone like this when her friend obviously belonged in bed?

"Of course I will," she replied bracingly. "There's bound to be a lot of young people on the bus and at the lodge, even though I *will* miss you. Now, I think you ought to hop into bed and take care of yourself. I'll call you when I get home, okay?"

Chris promised she'd take care, told her she'd be looking forward to her call, and then, before hanging up, wailed, "Oh, Jen, I was looking forward to this trip so much."

As she replaced the receiver Jen felt like wailing herself. The pleasurable glow that had filled her as she'd counted down the last few days had been extinguished with Chris's first words. What, she asked herself, did a young woman do on her own at a ski lodge? Never having been to a ski lodge, Jen didn't have the beginnings of an idea. But she

10

was sadly certain that the long four-day weekend was going to be a total disaster. Glancing at the clock, she gave a soft yelp and jumped up. If she didn't get moving she'd miss the bus, and she simply could not afford that.

Jen had a quick breakfast of toast and coffee, and moving quietly through the small ranch house so as not to waken her parents, she carried her second cup of coffee into her bedroom. Moving swiftly, she donned lacy minuscule panties and bra, stepped into designer boot jeans, pulled on buff-colored high-heeled suede boots, and slipped into a bulky knit, roll-collared sweater in a shade of rust that should have clashed with her flaming red hair but didn't.

After checking her soft white leather suitcase for the third time to make sure she hadn't forgotten anything, she locked it, tossed her key case into her shoulder bag lying on the bed, and headed for the bathroom on tiptoes to prevent her heels from clacking on the tiled hallway. All her tiptoeing and quiet moving around hadn't worked, for a light tapping sounded on the bathroom door as she put the finishing touches to her makeup.

"Are you just about ready, Jen?" Her mother's quiet voice filtered through the door. "It's twenty-five minutes after five."

"In a second," she called back softly. Her hand, poised to apply a strawberry scented lip gloss to her mouth, hovered as Jen grinned at her reflection. Would the day ever come when she could slip out of the house unheard by her mother? She hoped she'd never find herself in the position of wanting to elope for, short of crawling out of her bedroom window in her nightclothes, she'd never make it.

The gold-flecked hazel eyes in the mirror sparkled with laughter at the thought, while the full, beautifully shaped mouth grinned back at her, revealing good-sized white teeth with just a hint of an overbite. Composing her well-formed features, Jen smoothed on the gloss, stuck her

11

small pink tongue out at herself, and left the room. Her mother stood at the front door waiting for her, her suitcase beside her, her handbag in one hand and her ski jacket, purchased for this trip, in the other.

"You may break a leg," she said blandly as Jen reached for the jacket, "but at least I won't have to worry about you getting lost in the snow while you're wearing this beacon. I really think they saw you coming, Jennifer," she ended with a sad shake of her dark red head.

"Now, Mom, I was not sold a pig in a poke," Jen laughed softly, plucking the garment in question out of her mother's hand. "I loved it on sight and knew I had to have it." Shrugging into the shiny, bright red jacket with its hot pink stripes, Jen's laughter deepened as her mother squinted her eyes as if against a sudden glare. "And," she added with an impish grin, "as it was the only one like it they had in stock, I considered it a stroke of fortune that it was in my size."

"It will more likely give someone a stroke just looking at it," her mother quipped dryly. "Unless, of course, you keep dawdling. If you don't get a move on, you'll miss the bus."

"I'm going, I'm going," Jen laughed. Reaching for her handbag and suitcase at the same time, she planted a kiss on her mother's still smooth cheek, teased, "Be good," and slipping out into the cold morning, she sent a soft "You bet" over her shoulder in answer to her mother's cautioned "Take care, Jennifer."

Driving along the dark streets, Jen threw a reproachful look at the car's heater. *Why is it things always seem to go wrong the minute you pay something off?* She had made the final payment on the Mustang the month before and now, suddenly, in late January when she needed it most, the dratted heater had decided to be temperamental. Moments later she sent up a silent prayer that the windshield wipers had not contracted the no-work malady from the heater as a light misty rain clouded the window. Holding

12

her breath, she flicked the switch, then released her breath in a long sigh as the blades swished back and forth on the glass with reassuring regularity.

Stopping at a red light, Jen watched the wipers with a sinking sensation. *First Chris's call and now rain,* she thought dejectedly. *What next?*

Easing the car into motion again, she slanted a quick glance at her watch. Five thirty-five, and she should be at Barton's inside of ten minutes—plenty of time to make the bus.

Turning onto the road that lead to the large office complex, Jan sighed with relief at the sparsity of traffic at that hour of the morning. The macadam gleamed wetly in the beam from her headlights and at patches slick with a fine film of forming ice.

The tension of hard concentration eased somewhat when her lights touched the sign reading Barton's—Constructural Engineers, Inc. at the turnoff to the private road. The firm's parking lot comprised a large area, empty now but for the small group of cars parked at the far end.

Jen maneuvered the Mustang into a lined space beside a rather beat-up van and glanced around, wondering, *Where's the bus?*

At that moment, as if her thought was its cue, the large vehicle turned onto the parking lot and headed for the parked cars, its high, strong headlights bringing the small group into harsh relief.

Before the bus had come to a full stop, car doors were flung open, and the early-morning stillness was shattered by the sound of excited laughing voices as people left their cars and collected luggage. Following suit, Jen stepped out of the car, pulled her case from the back, and, depressing the lock button, swung the door to add to the cacophony of sound being made by the other doors being slammed shut.

Standing at the back of the line that had formed in front of the bus's open door, Jen caught snatches of the laughing

13

banter being tossed back and forth as the group waited for their names to be checked on the guide's roster and their luggage to be stashed in the large compartment on the side of the bus.

"Yeah, if she ever gets off the beginner slopes," one young man gibed.

"Right now the idea of a hot cup of coffee in front of a crackling fire sounds like heaven," a slim woman around forty laughingly told her tall, very thin male companion.

"This being engaged isn't all it's cracked up to be," the good-looking man directly in front of Jen said quietly to the equally good-looking man beside him. "Do you believe I had to swear I wouldn't look at another girl for the next four days?"

Hating to be an eavesdropper yet not knowing how to avoid it, Jen heard the other man ask softly, "Why didn't she come with you?"

"For one thing, she doesn't ski," the first young man replied disgustedly. "For another, she had to stay around this weekend as there's a shower planned for her. It's supposed to be a surprise, but she's known about it for weeks. Honestly, the games these women play are enough to drive a man to drink."

"Or to the ski slopes," the other man said, laughing softly.

The tiny smile that had begun to tug at Jen's lips disappeared when the man went on even more softly, "Of course, there are some games these gals play that drive a man to other things . . . I refer to bedroom games, naturally."

"Yeah, well, you can forget that once you've put the diamond on her finger," the first man murmured bitterly, taking a step as the line moved forward. "All of a sudden they become pure and want to wait. And that will drive a normal man over the edge completely."

Jen felt her cheeks grow warm in embarrassment, then

14

her spine stiffened in anger at the advice the man's friend proffered.

"Well, as I'm sure there'll be plenty of more-than-willing females at the lodge, you'll have four days to work off your frustrations."

Thankfully their conversation was terminated before the other man could reply, as they were given the okay to enter the bus. *Creeps,* Jen thought scathingly as she moved up to a young woman holding a clipboard in her hands.

"Are you Jennifer Lengle?" the harried young woman asked. At Jen's nod she went on, "I'm sorry Chris couldn't make it. There must be a bug going around. I had six cancellations besides Chris's this morning, including the travel agency's guide." Then, as the bus driver indicated he had her case, the woman said, "Oh, well, I'm sure you'll have a good time anyway, Jennifer. You can get on the bus now."

With a murmured "Thank you" followed by a shiver, Jen gladly took the high step up that took her out of the cold misty rain. Making her way slowly along the narrow aisle, Jen ignored an empty seat behind the ones occupied by the young men who'd stood in front of her in the line and stopped at double empties farther back in the bus. After sliding into the window seat, she placed her shoulder bag on the seat Chris would have occupied, then sat gratefully soaking in the warmth from the bus's powerful heaters.

Settling her long frame as comfortably as possible in the confined seating space, Jen let her eyes roam over her fellow passengers. How many, she wondered, were employees of the engineering firm and how many were guests? Like many similar firms, Barton's had an employees association that, with the help of a travel agency, planned several trips a year for employees and their guests. The destinations of these trips were well chosen, and they were amazingly reasonable in cost.

This particular tour to a ski lodge in the Adirondacks

15

in upper New York State was the first for Jen. Chris had taken advantage of several previous tour plans during the last few years. She had been to Williamsburg in Virginia; Mystic Seaport in Connecticut; New York City; and, the winter before, had enjoyed a skiing trip in Vermont. And on each occasion she had tried to coax Jen into going along. Jen would have loved to go, but somehow the trips had always seemed to be at times when she had other commitments. Chris had been delighted when Jen told her she could go on this trip. And they had talked of little else the last few weeks.

Sighing regretfully, Jen continued her perusal of the other passengers, hearing yet not registering their chatter. Although there were a few older people, it was, in the main, a young group, the females outnumbering the males almost two to one. Remembering the words about plenty of more-than-willing females the young man in the line had whispered to his friend, Jen grimaced. Promising herself she'd stay clear of that young man during the next four days, Jen dismissed him from her mind.

On the whole the group appeared open and friendly, calling to each other back and forth from one side of the bus to the other. There was no reason why she shouldn't enjoy herself, Jen mused. And there really was no reason why she should.

At twenty-three Jen was happy with her life and it showed. Her more than just pretty face, given a wholesome look by the fine sprinkling of freckles across her pert nose, glowed with good health. Her taller than average, somewhat lanky frame had the firm, supple appearance that comes from plenty of exercise. And her crowning glory was exactly that: a long, glorious mane of flaming red, wavy hair that framed her creamy-skinned face beautifully.

Content with herself and her life, Jen viewed the world serenely. Not subject to extreme emotional moods, she was usually pleasant and outgoing. In her position of private secretary to two struggling young lawyers, she had to deal with people, old and young, from all walks of life. She had been in the office less than a week when she'd decided that, by and large, most people were basically nice. The idea that she might be observing the world through rose-colored glasses never occurred to her.

Glancing at her watch, Jen frowned. It was already ten minutes after six. *What could the delay be for?* Shrugging mentally, she rested her head back against the seat. At that moment the murmured conversation in back of her erupted into laughter and movement, and in the action the hair at the back of Jen's head was ruffled.

"Oh, gosh, I'm sorry!" The contrite exclamation came from directly behind Jen.

An understanding smile curving her generous mouth, Jen twisted around in the high-backed seat.

"That's okay, no harm done," she assured the worried-faced girl leaning forward in her seat. About Jen's age, the girl was small and cute. The smile that replaced her concerned expression was singularly sweet. Bright blue eyes studied Jen a moment, lingering on her hair.

"Are you Chris Angstadt's friend Jen?" she asked in a surprised tone.

"Yes, I am." Jen's smile widened. "How did you know?"

"Oh, Chris has mentioned you a couple of times," she said, grinning. "And she has described your hair." The grin broadened. "It's pretty hard to miss. But where's Chris?" Her grin was replaced by a frown. "If she doesn't get here soon, the bus will go without her."

"She can't go," Jen sighed, then explained why.

"That's too bad. I know how excited she was about this trip." The girl shook her head, then added, "Oh, that means you're on your own." At Jen's nod she offered, "If you like, you can kinda hang around with us. I'm Lisa Banks, and this is Terry Gardner." With a wave of her hand she indicated the young woman in the seat beside her. "We work in the same department Chris does."

"Hi," Jen said, returning Terry's smile. "And thanks. You're sure I won't be intruding?"

"Of course not," Lisa laughed. "But Terry and I do have an agreement not to cramp each other's style if something interesting turns up."

"Something male, you mean?" Jen teased. She laughed softly as both girls nodded emphatically. "I'll go along with that agreement."

"That is if we ever get there," Terry grumbled. "What the heck are we sitting here for?"

Wondering the same thing, Jen turned to the front of the bus. At that moment Liz jumped up onto the high step. Shrugging disgustedly to the driver, she said tersely, "Go."

The door was closed, the air brakes were released, and the big vehicle began moving slowly across the parking lot. Before Liz could seat herself, her name was called from a half dozen voices back through the bus. As one of the voices belonged to Terry, Jen turned questioning eyes to her.

"Liz is the head of the committee that arranges these tours," Terry answered Jen's unasked query. "And I'll bet everyone wants to ask her the same thing: exactly what was the holdup?"

Liz made her way slowly down the aisle, stopping every so often to speak briefly before moving on again. When she reached the empty seat beside Jen she smiled ruefully and launched into an explanation.

"Sorry about the delay." Her sweeping glance included everyone on both sides of the aisle. "I was waiting for two people." She shrugged. "I don't know if they overslept or what, but we just couldn't wait any longer." She started to move on, then paused. "Oh, by the way, the rain has changed to snow. And the bus driver told me the last

18

weather report before he left the terminal called for snow all along the East Coast today."

All eyes, including Jen's, swung to the windows, but the darkness outside, combined with the tinted glass, made it impossible to see the fine snow.

"Well, if it's snowing out there," Lisa muttered, "it must be very fine. I'm darned if I can see it."

Fleetingly, Jen thought of her father's conviction that the bad snowstorms always start fine. *Oh, well,* she thought, and smiled at her reflection in the window, *where we're going snow is devoutly to be wished for.*

After turning onto the highway, the bus picked up speed. Depressing the button on the underside of her right armrest, Jen tilted her seat back, shifting into a reasonably comfortable position. The excited buzz of conversation swirled around her for several miles, then petered out. Lulled by the steady hum of the engine and the now low murmurings of the other passengers, Jen's eyes slowly closed.

A sudden jolting of the bus waked her. Sitting up stiffly, Jen gazed out the window at the gray morning. The snow could be seen now, still fine but falling steadily.

"Well, good morning, glory," Lisa chirped directly behind her. "I was going to give you a few more minutes and then wake you. We'll be stopping for breakfast soon."

"Mmmm—sounds good." Jen covered a yawn and glanced at her watch. "Good grief, I slept over an hour!"

"I think most everyone on the bus did," Terry informed her cheerfully. "They're just starting to come alive now."

"Probably hungry," Jen commented, sitting up straight to ease her cramped back.

Smoothing her tousled hair, she peered out the window. The highway, though wet and slick-looking, as yet had very little accumulation of snow. As she studied the road, a gold Formula drew alongside the bus. The rack mounted on the roof of the sporty-looking car held one pair of skis.

Someone else going skiing, Jen thought idly, staring into

the interior of the car. The passenger seat was empty, and all she could see of the driver was part of one pants-covered leg and one hand on the steering wheel. Oddly, the sight of that hand sent a funny tingle through Jen's middle. In the few seconds the car paced the bus, the look of that right hand was imprinted on her mind. It was a big hand, the back of it broad, and somehow Jen knew the fingers that curved firmly, confidently around the wheel were strong. Yet the exposed wrist was very narrow, deceptively delicate-looking. For one uncanny instant Jen thought she could actually feel the touch of that hand. She shivered as the car moved ahead, passing the bus.

Chiding herself for being fanciful, Jen pushed the image of that male hand from her mind. Liz's voice, heard clearly over the loudspeaker, helped to dispell the picture.

"Listen up, people," she quipped. "We'll be stopping for breakfast in a few minutes. I'd like to keep our stopping time to an hour or less, so please don't dawdle over your food."

While she was speaking, the bus driver drove off the highway into the parking area of a fairly large restaurant.

"Don't let the number of cars here upset you. We are expected, and everything should be set up for us. Please sign the check the waitress gives you and hand it to me before coming back to the bus. Thank you and enjoy your meal." With those final words Liz clicked the mike off and sat down.

Glancing out the window as the driver maneuvered the bus around the fringes of the lot, Jen caught sight of the ski-topped gold Formula parked near the front of the building. A picture of a hand flashed into her mind. Dismissing the tingle that came with the image, Jen smiled to herself. *Maybe now I'll be able to attach a body and face to the hand,* she reasoned in amusement.

On entering the restaurant, she was quickly disabused of that idea. The place was full, and the majority of the customers were men. Unless she could go from man to man examining right hands, Jen thought whimsically, she didn't have the slimmest chance of adding a body to that narrow-wristed appendage.

True to Liz's words, the restaurant's staff was expecting them, and they were swiftly herded into an empty dining room in the rear of the building. By the time Jen emerged from the building fifty minutes later, the Formula was gone, as she had been sure it would be.

On the move once more, Jen settled into her seat for the long ride ahead. Mesmerized by the now large white crystals swirling in a downward slant, Jen stared out the window. The farther north they went, the heavier the snow fell, in spots so thickly she could barely see the countryside.

A chorus of "Jingle Bells" rang out from the very back of the bus, and within seconds everyone had joined in. Everyone except the driver, whose eyes studied the highway carefully, a small frown beginning to draw his brows together.

They had sung their way robustly through "Winter Wonderland," "Let It Snow, Let It Snow," and even back to "Jingle Bells" when the first blast from the suddenly risen wind hit the bus broadside. Silence fell as a shudder rippled through the large vehicle.

"I hope she stays afloat."

The quip, from a deliberately dry male voice, produced the results intended. Female giggles and male laughter eased the tension that had blanketed the atmosphere. The second windy broadside was not as strong and so was met with complacency.

Jen's eyes had flown to the window at the first shock from the wind, widening in disbelief at the absolutely white world they encountered. Not only could she not see the countryside beyond the highway, she could not see the highway. Driven before the wind, the madly swirling snow, now falling heavily, had closed in on the bus, cutting visibility to zilch.

21

Growing uneasy, Jen kept her eyes fastened on the window even though she couldn't see much of anything. *Where exactly are we?* Biting her lip, Jen strained her eyes in an effort to see the surrounding terrain. She knew they were in New York State as she had seen the sign some distance back when they had crossed the line dividing New York and Pennsylvania. A third shudder shook the bus, and Jen's hands closed tightly on the armrests of her seat.

"This is beginning to give me the creeps," Lisa quavered behind Jen. "I know we're in some mountain range, and the last time I could see the road it appeared very narrow."

"If you're trying to scare me," Terry squeaked, "you're succeeding very well."

Jen was mentally agreeing when the bus swayed, the back end fishtailing as it was buffeted by a fresh assault from the wind. All conversation ceased abruptly, and Jen felt a shiver feather her spine at the frightened stillness. That the bus was obviously moving very slowly up an incline added to the apprehension growing among the passengers.

A collective sigh of relief was expelled as the bus reached the summit and leveled off. But the sigh was followed by another collective gasp as it started its descent down the other side.

"Oh, God!"

The softly exclaimed moan came from a woman toward the front of the bus. A moment later Liz's voice, her tone even and steady, came from the loudspeaker.

"Please remain calm. Our driver—whose name is Ted, by the way—has enough to contend with just keeping this bus on the road. As you can see, we're in the middle of a full-scale blizzard. Driving conditions are getting worse all the time. What we don't want here is panic. From my vantage point up here I can honestly tell you that Ted is doing one fantastic job of driving. You can all help him by staying calm. Now, are there any questions?"

22

There were a dozen questions, all babbled at once. The mike came back on with an angry click.

"One at a time, please," Liz snapped. "We'll have to use the schoolroom method of raised hands."

Over a dozen arms shot into the air; the question and answer period commenced.

"Are we going to have to turn back?" This from one of the men who'd stood in front of Jen in line.

Liz had a hurried, murmured conversation with the driver before answering.

"There is no decision on that yet." Liz held up her hand to stem the tide of comments that followed her statement.

"Here's the picture," she said sharply, effectively cutting through the rumble. "We've been in the thick of this storm for over two hours. The big question is: Which way is this hummer moving? If we keep going, can we drive out of it? If we turn back, can we drive out of it? We simply don't know the answer. Ted's going to pull into the first service station we come to and try and find out. Until then, we keep going."

While Liz had been speaking, the bus had inched down the descent and was now on a level road. There was quiet for several minutes. Then, from behind Jen, Terry asked, "Does it look as bad through the windshield as it does from these side windows?"

Every person on the bus heard Liz sigh.

"I won't try and con you," she said quietly. "It is grim. I don't know if anyone could see them, but we've already passed several cars that had pulled off the highway. Ted has a slight advantage in both the size of the bus and his elevated position."

The mike clicked off, and she leaned close to the driver. After long, tense moments the bus lurched off the highway to the tune of one sharp outcry and several gasps.

"Hold the phone, gang," Liz soothed. "We're pulling into a gas station."

The minute the bus came to a halt the driver was out

23

of his seat and through the door. At his exit the bus filled with sound. Everyone seemed to be talking at once.

Jen, sitting rigidly straight, peered wide-eyed out the window. She could see very little, but what she did see sent a shiver down her back. There were two cars parked haphazardly very near the bus, and she wondered in amazement how Ted had managed to avoid plowing into them as they were both nearly covered with drifted snow. The snow still fell heavily, spiraling in a wild and crazy dance before the wind.

"Scary, isn't it?" The frightened whisper came from Lisa.

Twisting around, Jen looked into the girl's pale face, knowing her own cheeks were as devoid of color.

"Yes," she murmured on an expelled breath.

Their driver was gone about ten minutes. On his return a waiting hush filled the bus. After a short conference with Liz, he took the mike from her and clicked it on.

"Okay, folks, here's the story." His brisk, confident tone went a long way in easing the almost tangible tension. "We are in a beauty. If you remember, Liz told you before we left Norristown that the report was for snow, but nothing like this. This storm ripped out of Canada and caught everyone with their pants down, so to speak."

A nervous twitter rippled through the bus.

"I think we should turn back," the woman across the aisle from Jen said loudly, nervously.

"We are not going to run out of it," Ted stated flatly. "At last report, this storm is dumping snow on the East Coast as far south as Virginia. Right now, apparently, the center of the storm is stalled over New York and Pennsylvania. The station owner has a C.B., and he just told me he's been picking up reports of stranded motorists both ahead and behind us. There are, in fact, three cars stranded here now."

"We're surely not going to stay here?" the same woman shrilled.

24

"No, we're not," Ted answered quietly.

Watching him closely, Jen decided she liked the driver's style. A man in his early forties, he had a tested, competent look that was reassuring. Still speaking quietly, he ignored the outburst that followed his last words and went on.

"The station owner said there is a motel fifteen to eighteen miles further along this road." Ted paused for breath, his face settling into a determined mask. "I'm going for it."

CHAPTER 2

Over an hour later, the large bus hardly seeming to move as it crawled along at a snail's pace, Jen observed the very stillness of her fellow passengers and smiled around the apprehension gripping her own throat. The nail-biting quiet had settled on the group when the bus had begun its slow crawl forward.

What amused Jen was the contrast between this very stillness and the furor that had erupted on Ted's stated "I'm going for it."

Those four small words had sparked off pandemonium, albeit a very short-lived pandemonium.

"I think we should stay here," the woman across the aisle from Jen shouted, conveniently forgetting she had moments before protested that very idea. A chorus of agreement followed the woman's agitated shout.

"I want to go home." This teary wail, which came from a young woman near the front, received a look of scorn from Ted. Yet, illogically, a chorus of agreement, mostly female, also followed that statement.

"Dammit, man," an angry male voice rose above the other voices, "you just finished saying there were motorists stranded all over these roads. Why take a chance on becoming one of them? I think the lady's right. We'd be safer staying right here."

Just about everyone on the bus joined in vocal agreement with that advice. Everyone, that is, except Jen, who sat in mute fascination watching Ted's face harden.

"I am responsible for this bus and everyone on it." Ted's cold tone, amplified by the loudspeaker, silenced the uproar. "The decision is mine and I've made it." An angry murmur rumbled through the bus, cut short by Ted's next words. "Now, if you'll be quiet, I'll explain why I made it."

Her respect for the man growing, Jen's eyes shifted to study the sullen but now quiet passengers. When her eyes swung back to the driver she had to gulp back a surprised "Oh." Unless she was seeing things, Ted had winked at her!

"Thank you," he drawled when the last mutter had died out. "The reason I'm going to try to reach that motel is for your safety and comfort. I've been in storms like this before. No one can ever predict their duration or severity. We could be held up for as little as one day. Or we could be stranded for as long as one week. Think about it."

As he paused to let his words register, Jen watched the faces of the people nearest to her change from indignation to fearful astonishment. She could almost hear the same words ringing in their minds that were echoing in hers. *One week!*

"Now"—Ted's calm voice drew their complete attention—"the reason I think I can make it is the obvious one, and that is simply the very size of this vehicle. This sucker can plow through much deeper snow than a car can. Also, as it carries a hell of a lot more fuel, I can take it slow without the fear of running out of gas. It may get a little hairy," he warned softly, then underlined firmly, "but I'll make it. No more questions. No more protests. I want it quiet as a church in here. We're moving."

With that he had clicked off the mike, slid into his seat, and after flexing his shoulders, move they did, very slowly, very carefully—forward.

Now, over a tension-filled, tautly quiet hour and a half later, the bus was still moving. They had had a few hairy moments. The worst was when a strong gust of wind had

27

caught the back end of the bus, sweeping it off the highway. Moans of fright and several screams had accompanied the bus's rocking swing. Thankfully Ted's cool actions and quick reflexes had brought the lumbering vehicle back under control and back onto the highway. At least what was assumed to be the highway by the occasional sign sticking up out of the deep snow that they passed.

Nervous perspiration beading her forehead, Jen, as frightened as everyone else, bit her lip against the demoralizing sounds of soft weeping that began suddenly with one woman and spread rapidly to others, including Lisa and Terry behind her. Nails digging into her palm, she hung onto her composure by hanging on to her faith in Ted.

Although there wasn't the slightest resemblance, he reminded Jen of her father. Like her father, Ted's quiet self-confidence instilled trust. Ralph Lengle was a taciturn, unassuming man who went about the business of getting a job done with tenacity. As she had inherited a strong streak of tenacity herself, Jen could recognize it in others. Ted had it.

The soft sobbing tearing at her emotions, Jen stared out the window with a new respect for the delicately formed crystals. They were pristine and pure, their white laciness beautiful, yet in accumulation, potentially treacherous. As, Jen mused, are many forms of nature unleashed in fury.

Eyes squinted against the continuing glare of white, Jen felt she'd lived through days as the seconds slowly slid into long, long minutes. God, if *she* felt exhausted, how must Ted be feeling by now? The thought drew her eyes to the not very broad but competent-looking back. The back moved as, hand over hand, the large steering wheel was turned and the bus lurchingly crossed the highway.

·"What now?" the woman across the aisle from Jen sobbed.

The mike clicked on as the bus came to a complete stop. Liz's voice had the breathy sound of released tension.

"We're home free, gang," she laughed tremulously. "We're at the motel."

As if pulled by an unseen cord, they all, Jen included, rose in their seats, necks craning to see out of the wide windshield. Sure enough, its large bulk looming darkly through the swirl of white, the motel stood a short distance before them.

Blinking against the hot surge of moisture that filled her eyes, trembling with reaction, Jen sank back in her seat, mentally issuing a prayer of thanks. The next moment her tear-bright eyes flashed in astonished disbelief at the stupidity of a wailed question that broke through the jerkily relieved, excited chatter.

"What do we do if they have no room and won't take us in?"

The shocked silence that followed that inanity told Jen she was not alone in her judgment of the woman's intellect.

"They will take us in." Ted's voice came cold and clear, without benefit of the loudspeaker. "Even if they are already packed." With a disgusted shake of his graying head he dismissed the subject, saying crisply, "Okay, gather whatever hand luggage or paraphernalia you may have with you and get ready to leave the bus. No one," he said sharply, "is getting off this bus until *everyone* is ready. That wind is mean, so I suggest you walk in twos and stay close together. The men will lead off in order to blaze a trail."

Ted waited until the general hubbub of preparation had died down, then said briskly, "All right, let's go."

The door opened, and the line that formed in the narrow aisle inched forward slowly. When she reached the front of the bus Jen was not surprised to see Ted, in snow nearly up to his knees, standing stoically beside the door, giving a helping hand to his alighting passengers. Grasping hands or arms, he assisted and steadied each successive person. When he turned to take Jen's outstretched hand a gentle smile touched his compressed lips. As she made the half step, half leap, into the snow, a strong gust of wind knocked her off balance. A strong hand at her back kept her from falling.

"Thank you," Jen laughed shakily.

"Thank *you*," Ted returned meaningfully.

Jen shot him a puzzled look, but he had turned to assist Lisa off the step. Hunching her shoulders against the biting force of the wind, she stood beside Lisa until Terry had joined them. Huddled together they made their way carefully along the uneven path in the snow, heads bent to protect their faces from the sting of the wind and the swirling wet flakes.

Blinking to dislodge some snow clinging to her lashes, Jen glanced up to see how much farther they had to go and felt her breath catch as her gaze encountered a partially snow-covered gold Formula, minus skis. Again a clear picture of that male right hand flashed into her mind. A shiver rippled through her body, and hunching her shoulders even more, Jen tore her eyes away from the car.

When they reached the covered entranceway to the building, they paused to brush the clinging snow from each other before entering the roomy lobby. Joining the rest of their group, standing together off to one side, they were informed that Liz was at the reception desk inquiring about rooms. Ignoring the laughing, excited chatter around her, Jen's eyes took stock of the motel.

It was obviously newly built; Jen labeled the decor plushy rustic. Curving open staircases, one at either side of the lobby, indicated the motel had two floors and that the rooms were reached from inside passageways. Jen registered that fact with a sigh of relief; at least they wouldn't have to plow to rooms with outside entrances. To her right, under the curve of the staircase, an archway with louvered swinging doors led into what Jen could see was the bar. Facing it across the width of the lobby, a matching archway led into a dining room, empty now and only dimly lit. To the rear two similar but smaller archways, without swinging doors, led into what Jen thought were hallways. Liz's voice drew Jen's attention from the large wagon wheel style chandelier hanging by a thick chain from the high open-beamed ceiling.

"Can I have your attention, please?" The sound of metal clinking against metal followed her words as Liz lifted a handful of room keys. "As you can see, they were able to accommodate us. As a matter of fact we've taken the last rooms available." She paused to allow the spattering of relieved comments, then said crisply, "Now, as I call your names, please step forward for your key."

The ensuing procedure was by necessity a slow one as Liz had to check and mark her clipboard after each key was handed out. When she got to Lisa and Terry, who had planned to share a room—as Jen and Chris had—she paused before glancing up at Jen.

"Jennifer, you are going to have to bunk with Lisa and Terry. I'm sorry, but"—she shrugged—"that's the only way we can get everyone in."

"It beats sleeping on the bus," Jen quipped dryly, stepping forward to join Lisa and Terry.

"No big deal," Lisa grinned. "Unless you snore, that is."

Key in hand, Lisa lead the way to the stairway to their right. At the top of the stairs she swung down the hallway, checking room numbers on both sides against the one on the key tag. When she reached the one that matched, she unlocked the door, pushed it open and, with a sweeping wave of her hand, ushered Jen and Terry in with a chirped, "It may get crowded, but it shouldn't get dull."

The large room contained two double beds covered with patchwork spreads, a matching pair of molded plastic chairs in burnt orange placed one on either side of a tole metal floor lamp and a long combination dresser-desk against the long wall. A color TV with FM connection sat on the end of the low dresser closest to the chairs. The bathroom was tiled in rust, the fixtures and molded Fiberglas tub-shower combination in white.

After they finished examining their temporary domain, Terry dropped onto the bed, declaring she was going to have a delayed nervous breakdown and then a nap. Grinning while she tugged her sweater over her head, Lisa opted for a hot shower.

Standing at the mirror, trying to brush her damp, curly mane into some sort of order, Jen said seriously, "Being scared always dries me up. I feel parched, so I think I'll investigate that bar downstairs." Dropping the brush onto the dresser, she scooped up her handbag and left the room.

Jen pushed through the swinging doors, then paused to take a quick inventory of the room, which was full. The end of the room closest to the entrance contained a large horseshoe-shaped bar manned by three barmaids. The center section contained a dozen or so tables covered with patchwork cloths and topped by candles set inside dark red glass globes. The far end of the room was set up as a lounge area with a long, low-backed sofa and several overstuffed chairs grouped around a wide fireplace in which a real fire flickered and sent out long fingers of orange-red light.

Laughter and conversation vied with the music from the jukebox. Unable to see one unoccupied seat, Jen sighed and was about to leave when she saw a raised arm beckon her to the bar.

Following the curving bar to the still-raised arm, a smile lit Jen's face when she saw the arm belonged to Ted.

Ignoring a softly called "Hi, honey, looking for me?" from a man four stools away from Ted, Jen made for the one and only empty seat in the place next to Ted.

"I believe just about everyone from the bus is in this place," Jen grinned as she slid onto the stool. "That was

32

some fancy piece of driving you did, sir. But very, very scary."

"I know, I'm still shaking," Ted grinned back, holding up an exaggeratedly trembling hand for proof. "What would you like to calm your nerves?"

"A glass of white wine, please," Jen told the hovering barmaid. Then, her face and tone serious, she looked into Ted's craggy face and murmured, "I knew you could make it."

The lines radiating from Ted's eyes crinkled as he smiled gently at her. "And I knew you felt I could," he said surprisingly. "Your confidence and trust in me was written on your face. I could read it all the way up front. It's a look I've been blessed with on occasion from my teen-age daughter."

"And I was thinking how much your determination reminded me of my father," Jen smiled back.

During their exchange Jen barely noticed that the man on the other side of Ted vacated his seat or that another had claimed it. But she did hear the deep, attractive voice that asked Ted if he was the driver of the bus in the parking lot.

Ted turned to answer in the affirmative, adding that after the ride he'd had that day, he might just look for a desk job. Ted's dry remark drew soft laughter from the unseen man, then Jen's heart thumped as a right hand was extended and the deep voice offered, "Adam Banner, and I know how you feel. I also drove through that mess."

"Ted Grayson," Ted replied, grasping the offered hand. "And this is Miss—?" Leaning back, Ted raised his brows at Jen.

"Jennifer Lengle," Jen supplied somewhat breathlessly, finding herself staring into a pair of eyes the color of dark brown velvet.

The sight of his hand on the steering wheel had sent a tingle through Jen; the look of him set off a clamor. He was perhaps the most attractive man she had ever seen.

His hair, though straight, was thick and full. The color reminded Jen of her morning toast, not dark enough to be brown, not light enough for blond. His features were even and regular, the jawline firm, determined. Dark brows slashed in an almost straight line above eyes heavily fringed with thick, dark lashes. And those eyes. If one were to imagine liquid velvet, Jen thought, bemused, it would look exactly like those eyes.

"How do you do, Miss Lengle?" His soft voice tugged at her wandering thoughts. "May I call you Jennifer?"

I'd rather you call me darling. The sudden thought shocked Jen, and yet it was true! She had never seen this man before. For all she knew he could be a criminal—or worse. But on his lips her name had sounded like a caress, and she felt a longing deep inside to hear that soft voice murmur an endearment. This feeling, never before experienced, confused and unnerved her. His soft questioning eyes brought her to her senses.

"M-my friends—everyone calls me Jen," she blurted, feeling her face grow warm.

"I think I prefer Jennifer." Sharp now with consideration, his eyes probed her pink cheeks.

Tearing her gaze from his, Jen clutched the glass of wine the barmaid had moments before placed in front of her and, bringing it to her lips, drank thirstily.

"I like Jen, myself," Ted opined teasingly. "It goes with the freckles."

It was obvious from Ted's easy, unaffected manner that he had missed Jen's slight stammer, the quickened sharpness of Adam's eyes. Had she imagined it? Jen asked herself. Had that electrical tautness that had seemed to sizzle between them been in her mind? She had to find out. The glass still at her lips, she turned her head very slowly, looking at him through the lashes of her demurely lowered lids.

He was waiting for her. The moment her glance touched him, he lifted his glass in silent acknowledgment and drank with deliberation and meaning, his eyes a warm caress on her face. *Zing.* The current ran, swift and hot, from his eyes to hers and down through her entire body, setting off sparks all along the way.

"It's stopped snowing, Ted."

The voice belonged to Liz. Dragging her gaze from Adam's, Jen turned to find the young woman at her shoulder, facing Ted.

"Some of the people from the bus have asked about their luggage." Liz grimaced ruefully. "I was delegated to come ask you if you could possibly unload it."

"What a bunch of sweethearts," Ted groaned. "I'll go take a look-see after I've finished my drink." Lifting his hand he motioned to the barmaid. When the mobcapped woman came to a stop across the bar, he asked, "What'll you have, Liz?"

"A Bloody Mary," Liz replied grimly. "I need something strong to wash the bad taste away. Every tour I've been on has been the same. The majority of the people are pleasant and easy to get along with, but there are always a few who simply can't be pleased."

The barmaid came back carrying the scarlet concoction, and Ted made a move to get up. Adam moved faster. Sliding off his stool, he reached around Ted and touched Liz on the arm.

"Have a seat and forget all of them for a while—Liz?" His brows went up questioningly.

"Yes—Liz Dorn, and thank you, Mr.—?"

"Banner, Adam—and you're welcome."

The smile he gave Liz caused an odd, sharp little pain in Jen's throat. Glancing away quickly, Jen studied the stemmed wineglasses hanging upside down on a round rack above the space behind the bar. *What in heaven's name is the matter with me?* Jen felt actually envious of Liz because of a smile. *This is insane,* she berated herself, gulping the last of her wine. *You don't even know the man.*

"Would you like another?"

Adam's warm, whiskey-scented breath feathered her cheek. Jen had to clamp her teeth together to keep from trembling.

"I—I don't think I'd better." Jen swallowed back a groan of self-disgust. *God, did that stammered, garbled reply make any sense at all?* Drawing a quick breath, she went on more slowly, "I haven't eaten since we stopped for breakfast, and I'm afraid another would go to my head."

As a matter of fact, she added silently, *I'm afraid the one drink has gone to my head.* Could that be it? Could it be the wine causing this funny squiggly feeling in her stomach and not the man? He was standing behind her, very close, and Jen suddenly felt hot. Yet the fingers that played with the stem of her glass were like ice.

"You're right," Adam agreed. "It's not a good idea to drink on an empty stomach."

"Speaking of empty stomachs," Ted sighed resignedly, standing up, "I guess everybody's is, and as they'll probably want to shower and change before dinner, I suppose I'd better see about unloading the luggage."

"I'll go with you," Adam volunteered. He finished his drink in a few deep swallows. "Coming, Liz?" Leaning forward, he placed his glass on the bar. Turning to look at her, he murmured, "Jennifer?"

Jen's pulses leaped, pushing her spirits up out of the disappointed low they'd slumped into at his offer to help. Like a magnet, his eyes drew her off the stool. And like a puppet whose strings he controlled, she followed him out of the room, Liz at her side.

At the wide glass double entrance doors they stood side by side, Ted, Adam, Jen, and Liz. The motel's bright outside lights bathed the parking area in a glow that shot glittering blue-gold reflections off the snow.

"It looks like a Christmas card," Jen said softly.

"Oh, yes," Liz breathed. "Isn't it beautiful?"

"And cold," Ted grumbled. "And wet."

36

The deep chuckle from beside Jen ricocheted along her nerve endings.

"We're not going to get it done standing here looking at it," Adam drawled. "It would be a lot easier if you could bring that monster closer to the entrance. What do you think, Ted, want to give it a try?"

"If you can get it up here, just let it sit after it's empty."

All four turned to stare at the small man who had spoken with authority. Thin and balding, the man was about fifty, with a pleasant smile and shrewd, intelligent eyes.

"Bill Wakefield," he smiled, showing white, even dentures. "I'm the manager here."

"Ted Grayson," Ted said.

"Adam Banner," Adam smiled. "And this is Liz Dorn and Jennifer Lengle."

Handshakes were exchanged and Bill Wakefield, his smile wry, repeated, "If you can get it up, leave it sit. I don't suppose we'll be getting any more customers tonight. I'll put a man to work with the snow blower in the front. If you can get the luggage unloaded, we'll have to carry it in ourselves. I'm working with a skeleton crew, as some of my day people went home early, and most of the evening shift didn't make it in."

"Well, I may as well get my jacket and get at it."

Ted turned and strode across the lobby, Adam right behind him.

Feeling completely useless, Jen stood watching as the motel employee began blowing the drifted snow under the covered entranceway. A light touch on her arm drew her attention from the gleam of white.

"Here's Ted and Mr. Banner," Liz said quietly. "It was very nice of him to offer to help Ted."

"Yes, he seems like a nice guy." Jen forced a note of lightness around the sudden tightness in her throat caused by the sight of Adam walking toward them.

What was it about this man that affected her so strongly? True, he was exceptionally good-looking, but Jen was past the age of being impressed by mere good looks. No, it was more—much more—than looks. But what?

Her expression carefully controlled, Jen watched him approach, her breath catching at a sudden leap of excitement inside. He was not even looking at her as he fastened the zipper closing of the dark brown and white ski parka he'd donned, a simple procedure made difficult because he carried a knitted cap in one hand and gloves in the other. The closing made, he glanced up, and Jen felt warmth radiate through her body as his eyes captured hers. He didn't say anything as he passed her and pushed through the heavy doors. But then he didn't have to say anything, for Jen received the message his eyes flashed to her as clearly as if he'd shouted it. The message was: Don't go away, wait for me here.

Shaken and confused by the strange telepathic experience, Jen's eyes followed his retreating back as, side by side, he and Ted plowed slowly through the knee-high snow. Without consciously trying to do it, Jen's mind sent out a plea to him of its own. Please be careful, and hurry back to me. That shook her even more.

She knew they had reached the bus when two bright lights, looking like the eyes of a huge monster, cut through the blackness that was the parking lot. Barely breathing, she watched those eyes move very, very slowly toward her. Suddenly those headlights blinded her, and with a small gasp she stepped back as the bus, looming out of the darkness, came directly at her. Then the lights arched away as the bus made a lurching swing and came to a stop parallel to the motel's entrance.

The moment the bus came to a halt Adam leaped agilely from the high step onto the now cleared area alongside which the vehicle had stopped. Ted was right behind him, keys dangling from his hand. The door of the storage compartment was opened, and the two men began hauling out the luggage.

"I think I'll go roust some of the men out of the bar to help," Liz declared in sudden decision. "Why should those two do all the work? Hell, Adam isn't even one of the passengers."

"Liz, wait," Jen's hand caught Liz's arm as she spun away. "If you go in there and call for assistance and they all troop out here, you're going to have nothing but mass confusion."

A rattling sound drew Jen's attention, and glancing across the lobby, she saw Bill Wakefield pushing a large luggage rack before him. Releasing Liz's arm, Jen walked to the doors, pushed through, then held it for Bill.

"Come on, Liz," she called. "If you and I help, we can have the bags loaded and inside in no time. Then you can call the others to the lobby to pick up their cases."

Jen didn't wait for a yes or no from Liz. Grabbing the front end of the rack, she guided it through the doors and over the cleared cement to the steadily growing pile of luggage. The night air was cold and damp, and Jen began shivering before she reached the pile of cases. Her teeth clenched together to keep them from chattering, she began stacking the cases onto the rack following Bill's directions, grinning at Liz who had followed her out.

Jen knew the bus was empty when the compartment door slammed shut. Five pairs of hands made short shrift of the job. Jen was reaching for one of the few remaining cases when strong, gloved hands grasped her shoulders, turning her to the doors.

"We'll finish up and bring it in," Adam said firmly. "You're cold—go inside. You too, Liz."

Although his tone was mild, it was an order. Without protest Jen and Liz obeyed. Standing inside the doors, Jen watched as the three men maneuvered the ungainly rack across the cement. She was shivering again, only now it was from the touch of those leather-covered hands, not the cold.

Clipboard in hand, Liz checked the tags on the bags

against the names on her list as Jen and the men unloaded the rack in front of the reception desk. When the conveyance was once again empty and the cases lined up into neat rows, Ted straightened.

"Thanks," he stated simply, then, his tone lightening, he asked, "How about having dinner together?"

"You're on," Liz said at once.

Jen, hesitating, glanced quickly at Adam, who nodded briefly at her before facing Ted.

"Sounds good." His gaze shifted back to Jen. "Jennifer?"

"Y-yes, of course," Jen agreed in a wavery voice. Why? Oh, why did the sound of her name on his lips unnerve her so?

"And I'll go and put a reserved sign on a good table for you," Bill said, heading for the dining room.

"Well," Liz sighed resignedly, "I guess I'll go call the thundering herd out of the bar." She started off, then glanced back. "Jen, would you go tell Lisa and Terry their bags are in the lobby?"

"Will do," Jen answered, reaching for her own bag.

Scooping her case from under her fingers, Adam said, "I'll take them. Which ones belong to the other two girls?"

Ignoring her protests, he clamped a case under one arm and picked up the other.

"What time should we meet for dinner?" Jen's eyes shifted from one to the other.

Ted shot a glance at his watch.

"Seven okay?" At Jen and Adam's nod, he added, "We can meet in the bar. I'll tell Liz."

As they walked up the stairs, Adam slanted Jen a teasing grin.

"I think there's something developing between Liz and Ted; I can feel the vibes."

"But he's married!" Jen exclaimed, shocked. "He told me he has a daughter."

"He's a widower," Adam corrected gently.

"But how do you kn—"

"I asked him, while we were in the bus, if he'd gotten a call through to his wife," Adam answered before she'd even finished asking. "He told me his wife was dead, but that he had reached his daughter."

"And do you really think there is something brewing between him and Liz?"

They had reached the room Jen was sharing with Lisa and Terry. Adam deposited the cases at the door before answering her question with one of his own.

"Haven't you seen the way they look at each other?"

"No." Jen shook her head.

"Well, I have." Adam's eyes stared straight into hers and the expression in them dried all the moisture in her mouth. When he spoke again she knew he was no longer talking about Liz and Ted.

"Every glance is a touch, a caress," he murmured. Turning away, he tacked on, "I'll see you at seven and—Jennifer—don't look so frightened."

CHAPTER 3

The hot, stinging spray from the shower overcame the chills that had attacked Jen's spine at Adam's parting words.

"Oh, glory," she groaned softly. "What is happening to me?"

The sound of her own voice, intensified by bouncing off the rust-colored tiles, startled her and brought her up short. *Good grief! Now I'm talking to myself,* she thought wearily. *But, what is happening to me?* Nothing like this had ever happened to her before.

Oh, sure, she had been attracted to other young men— as well as repelled—on first meeting. But this confusing clamor of emotions and senses, this all-over warm sensation while chills skipped down her spine, this scary, exciting desire to hear him say her name, to feel his eyes on her, was beyond understanding, beyond reason.

Jen dressed slowly and carefully in a room that was, finally, blessedly quiet. Lisa and Terry had left moments before, going down to the dining room to eat and, as Terry put it, "To check out the male prospects of the motel's inhabitants."

Thankfully, her breathless, flustered state on entering the room had been overlooked by the other two girls simply because she had kept her head down while dragging the cases inside. On seeing their luggage, both girls had jumped up with squeals of delight and began unpacking at once.

"I wonder if this is worth the effort," Lisa had mused, shaking out a frilly blouse before draping it carefully on a hanger. "Do you think there's any chance of going on to the resort tomorrow, Jen?"

"Well, it has stopped snowing, but"—Jen shook her head—"I doubt it. From what I could see of the parking lot, the snow looks pretty deep. I can't imagine what the roads are like."

"But suppose we unpack and they decide to go on tomorrow," Terry groaned. "We'll have to repack everything."

"I'm going to play it safe," Jen grinned. "I'm going to hang up the things that will crush and leave everything else in the case."

Lisa and Terry opted to do the same, and confusion reigned for several minutes as the three girls bumped into each other while moving back and forth between their cases and the room's one clothes closet.

"Would you like us to wait for you, Jen?" Lisa had called through the bathroom door as Jen prepared to take a shower.

"No, thanks, Lisa," Jen called back. "I'm having dinner with Liz and Ted." She hesitated, then added, "And a man we met in the bar."

"A man!" Lisa shrieked. "What man? Is he good-looking? Was he alone or was he with friends? Oh, why didn't I go down to the bar with you instead of—"

Jen had turned the shower on, effectively drowning out Lisa's voice. By the time Jen walked out of the bathroom Lisa and Terry had gone.

Now, putting the finishing touches to her makeup, a smile twitched at Jen's lips on remembering Lisa's questions. By the number of males evident in the bar, she thought wryly, Lisa should have no trouble finding company.

Stepping back to get a long view of herself in the mirror, Jen studied her reflection critically. Her long skirt, in a heather, lilac, and pale blue plaid, clung just enough to give her a leggy look. And her pale blue full-sleeved blouse in a soft, clingy material molded her high, full breasts while still managing to give her a somewhat fragile appearance.

With a nod of satisfaction she flipped back a fiery red tendril that insisted on falling across her cheek, picked up her handbag, and walked out of the room, breathing slowly to combat the excitement tickling her throat.

As she had a few hours earlier, Jen paused inside the swinging doors of the bar's entrance, stepping to one side to allow an approaching man to exit. The man drew alongside her, hand raised to push open the doors. The hand dropped as turning to her he asked, "Aren't you on the Barton's bus?"

"What?—oh, yes." Jen had barely noticed him as her eyes had been busy searching for Adam. A smile curving her lips, she turned to face him. The smile wavered, but she managed to keep it in place. It was the man who had stood in front of her in line that morning—could it have only been that morning?—the one who had advised his friend to work off his frustrations.

"Well, hi." His right hand was extended. "I'm Larry Gordon."

It was the first really good look she had of him. Larry Gordon was an exceptionally attractive young man, almost pretty. About twenty-five or six, he had a head full of soft blond curls that perfectly topped his boyishly innocent, baby blue-eyed face. His smile was warm, somewhat shy, and his eyes were guileless. If Jen had not overheard his words that morning, heard the underlying disdain for women in his tone, she'd have trusted him on sight. But she had heard him; she didn't trust or like him.

After a brief hesitation while these thoughts flashed through her mind, she placed her palm against his.

"Jen Lengle."

Maybe it was foolish, but Jen had a sudden aversion to

44

giving him her full name. After hearing Adam say it, she simply did not want it on this man's lips.

"Hello, Jen Lengle." His tone had a hint of intimacy that stiffened Jen's spine. "Since we both seem to be alone, how about having dinner with me?"

Good heavens! Jen thought in amazement. *Don't tell me his companion has found a playmate already?* Revulsion, combined with a hot shaft of anger, shot through her. Masking her face to keep it from showing, Jen felt her smile beginning to dissolve.

"I'm sorry, I'm meeting—" Jen began firmly, but a feathering shiver withered the refusal in her mouth. Her back to the bar as she faced Larry, she had not seen Adam cross the room, yet she knew he was there; the shiver told her.

"I've been waiting for you." Adam's quiet tone doubled her shivers. "Ted and Liz have gone into the dining room. As soon as you've introduced me to your friend, we'll join them."

Startled by the edge his tone had taken on, Jen's eyes flew to his face. His visage revealed nothing of what he was thinking, and his eyes looked flat, lifeless.

"Oh, yes—of course." Jen paused to draw a quick breath. What was the matter with her? She felt like a tongue-tied teen-ager caught in some guilty act. Guilty? For talking a few minutes with Larry? But why? The questions zapped through Jen's mind in the instant required to draw that calming breath. "Adam, this is Larry Gordon. He's one of the tour passengers. Larry, Adam Banner."

While the two men shook hands, exchanging the usual trite introductory conversation, Jen brought herself under control. Guilty indeed! But Adam's sudden appearance while she'd been talking to Larry had caused the strangest feeling, almost as if she were being disloyal. And she'd met Adam only a few hours ago! The word *strange* didn't seem strong enough.

45

Preoccupied with her confusing thoughts, Jen smiled vaguely at Larry when he excused himself and headed back to the bar, missing entirely the suggestive wink he sent her once he was beyond Adam's sight.

"Are you hungry?" Adam's quiet voice nudged her out of her musings.

"Starving." Jen walked by the door he was holding for her. "Are you?" she asked when he fell into step beside her.

"Yes," he answered shortly.

They were a few feet from the swinging doors into the dining room when Adam stopped moving and turned to her, a frown creasing his brow.

"Did you want to have dinner with him?"

Caught unaware by the abruptness of his query, Jen stared at him in perplexity. "With whom? Larry?" At his nod, she frowned. "Of course not."

"Good." The emphatic word seemed to be issued with a sigh of relief. Taking her arm, he started moving again. "Do you know him well?" His tone was even, bland. Almost too bland.

"I don't know him at all." Jen preceded him into the dining room with a smile of thanks as he again held the door. "And I don't want to know him," she added emphatically.

Adam lifted a hand to acknowledge Ted's beckoning wave from the corner of the room, while at the same time he lifted questioning brows at her.

"He comes on a little too strong," Jen answered his curious look.

"Has he been annoying you?" he asked sharply.

"Not at all!" Jen exclaimed, startled by the fierceness of his tone. Returning Ted and Liz's smiles as they approached the table, Jen added in an undertone, "But I know the type and I don't appreciate them."

The table Bill had kept for them was at the very end corner of the crowded room at a large plate glass window.

46

Every table was occupied, and the conversation and occasional laughter that floated on the air had a festive holiday ring.

Ted and Liz seemed to be in a festive mood as well. Liz looked decidedly sexy in an ice blue satin jumpsuit. Ted, out of uniform, looked younger and casually terrific in a patterned cream and tan knit pullover and dark brown slacks. With the weight of responsibility lifted from his shoulders, Ted was in a relaxed, teasing mood.

"What do you think, Adam?" he asked with feigned seriousness, his eyes moving from Liz to Jen. "Was it fate or pure blind luck that put us in the bar at the perfect time to latch onto the two loveliest women in this place?"

A slow, heart-stopping smile curved Adam's lips, and the warm velvet look was back in the eyes that followed Ted's from one pink-cheeked face to the other.

"I think it was a combination of both," Adam said softly. "A combination I have no desire to question but a strong desire to savor."

Jen felt her flush deepen under his melting gaze, felt her breath quicken as that gaze moved over her slowly, lingering first on her gently heaving breasts, then on her slightly parted lips.

God! He was making love to her with his eyes! Boldly, brazenly, in front of anyone who cared to watch, he was staking a silent claim on her. The response that quivered through Jen shocked her. Shaken by the intensity of her reaction to him, she tore her eyes away in embarrassment.

Incredibly, Liz and Ted seemed not to have noticed anything unusual. On closer inspection Jen decided it wasn't all that incredible, as Ted and Liz had eyes only for each other.

Aware now, attune to the vibrations, Jen, unable to tear her eyes away, watched the silent byplay between Ted and Liz. Ted's eyes, older but no less dimmed than Adam's, caressed her. Liz's reaction was much the same as Jen's had been.

What in the world was happening to all of them? The thought shot through Jen's mind like an outcry. Did being snowbound affect the mind, the senses? Feeling suddenly like an intruder, Jen lowered her eyes to the table. The tug of warm velvet drew her eyes from the Wedgwood blue tablecloth to Adam's face. His expression was both understanding and compassionate. He *knew* the turmoil and confusion she was experiencing!

The appearance of their waiter shattered the intimacy that seemed to encompass the table.

"Good evening, folks." The young man smiled pleasantly. "Would you like something from the bar before ordering?"

"I'll have a double martini on the rocks," Liz replied in a strained, breathless blurt.

Although Ted's eyebrows went up, an indulgent smile tugged at his lips.

"I'll have the same," he told the waiter.

"Jennifer?" Adam nudged at her hesitation. "White wine?" She nodded and he turned to the waiter. "And I'll have a Manhatten—with a twist."

"Yes, sir." With another quick smile the young man handed menus around, then sauntered away.

Quiet prevailed for several minutes while they studied the bill of fare, then, closing the menu, Liz said stiltedly, "I think I'll have the shrimp cocktail and the flounder stuffed with crab meat."

"The shrimp cocktail sounds good," Ted agreed, "but I'll go with the broiled scallops." Glancing first at Jen then at Adam, he asked, "What about you two?"

"French onion soup."

Their replies came simultaneously and, strangely, broke the tension simmering among all of them.

"And?" Ted laughed.

"Prime rib with baked potato." Jen grinned at Ted before prompting teasingly, "Adam?"

Broad shoulders inside a very expensive-looking off-white cable knit sweater lifted in a believe-it-or-not shrug.

"The same," he drawled softly.

The food was expertly prepared and delicious. Adam had cause to execute that elegant shrug once again when, taking the small boat of sour cream with chives Jen handed to him, he proceeded to pile every bit as much of it onto his potato as she had.

On leaving the dining room they encountered Bill Wakefield in the lobby and in a chorus congratulated him on his chef. Bill's slender face beamed at their lavish praise.

"Glad you enjoyed it and I'll be happy to pass your kind words on to the cook. It'll make his day." His smile turned impish. "Even though he knows he's good. Doesn't hesitate to tell me—regularly."

A phone rang, and from behind the registration desk the clerk called, "Phone for you, Bill."

"Coming," Bill called. "Enjoy yourselves." Then he added over his shoulder, "Oh, yeah, there's dancing in the bar tonight—to the jukebox."

"Well, at least the phones weren't knocked out of service," Liz observed as they strolled across the lobby.

"I never thought of that!" Jen exclaimed, stopping dead. "Look, you three go on ahead. I'm going to call home and let my parents know I'm all right and where I am."

It wasn't until the phone at her home was ringing that Jen realized she didn't know exactly where she was, and she couldn't ask the desk clerk as he'd disappeared on some errand. Her mother answered on the third ring.

"It's Jen, Mom. I just called to let you know I'm okay."

"Oh, Jen," Ella Lengle's voice sighed with relief. "We've been so worried. Are you at the lodge?"

"No, we're at a motel," Jen said ruefully. "But don't ask me where. All I can tell you is we're in New York State. Is it bad at home?"

"Yes," her mother sighed again. "We've been listening to the radio, and reports of power and phone lines going down are beginning to come in. Everything has come to a standstill, and the call has gone out for volunteers with four-wheel drive vehicles for emergencies."

"Well, it has stopped snowing here," Jen reported. "Maybe we'll be able to go on to the lodge tomorrow. We can't be too far from there. I'll call you in the morning and let you know."

After hanging up the phone, Jen walked to the entrance of the bar, stepped inside, and for the third time that day, paused while her eyes went skimming over the room. Beyond the bar a partitioning wall had been folded back to reveal a small dance floor, which was already full of couples gyrating to an upbeat tune throbbing from a large jukebox in the corner.

The bar was solidly packed two deep, although there were still several empty tables in the center of the room. Peering through the pall of gray smoke in the dimly lit room, a smile touched Jen's lips as her attention was caught by an upraised arm in the lounge area. The arm went higher into the air as Ted rose from the long, low-backed sofa. Waving back to him, Jen started toward the lounge area. Halfway across the room her name was called, and Jen glanced to her right to smile and wave at Lisa and Terry. When she turned back she found her way blocked by Larry Gordon.

"You're going in the wrong direction."

"What?"

"The dance floor is behind you," Larry smiled, revealing even white teeth. "You *are* going to dance with me, aren't you?"

"I've just finished eating and I'm too full to dance," Jen hedged, deciding she disliked this cocky young man more with each meeting.

"Then come to the bar and have a drink with me," he

ordered smoothly. "Then after your dinner settles, we'll dance."

For several seconds Jen stared at him in amazement. *Is this guy for real?* And was she actually supposed to be impressed by his takeover attitude? Biting back the scornful laugh that rose to her lips, she began softly, "I don't want—"

"Of course you do," he smiled insinuatingly, taking a step closer to her.

Fighting the urge to step back, Jen held her ground, lifted her chin, and insisted firmly, "No, thank you, I—" The words dried on her lips and her body stiffened as a hand curved around her waist from behind. The stiffness drained out of her with a warm rush of relief at the quiet yet commanding sound of Adam's voice.

"Back off, fella."

Larry's eyes flickered, and he did take one backward step before he caught himself in retreat and straightened with a fatalistic shrug.

"Sorry, man," he grinned knowingly. "Didn't mean to cut into your time." He started forward, and Jen turned aside to allow him to pass. As he did his arm deliberately brushed her breast, and he whispered, "Later, honey."

Not wanting to create a scene, Jen, swallowing the furious gasp that rose in her throat, glanced at Adam to see if he'd heard Larry's whispered gibe. It was more than obvious that he had, for his face was set in lines of cold rage and his eyes glittered dangerously from behind narrowed lids.

"That son-of-a—"

"Ignore him." Jen cut swiftly across his softly growled words. "Adam, please," she added urgently as his hand dropped from her waist, and he made a move to follow Larry. It was only when she shifted to stand in front of him that she saw he was holding a bar tray in his other hand. On the tray was a carafe of white wine and four stemmed glasses. The glasses shivered on the tray, alerting

Jen to the intensity of the anger rippling through Adam's body.

"Adam—"

It was a whispered plea, and with a sigh of relief Jen saw the glasses become still an instant before he tore his fierce gaze from Larry's back and focused on her upturned face.

"Ted and Liz are waiting for their wine," she said softly.

"If he touches you again, I'll—"

"He's not worth getting worked up over." Again she deliberately cut into his harsh tone. "And we're beginning to look conspicuous standing here." She laughed. "Don't you think we should join Ted and Liz?"

"Okay," he sighed, an answering smile twitching his lips.

Ted and Liz were ensconced at one end of the sofa, so deep in conversation they had apparently not even noticed Jen's delay in reaching them.

"Your wine, sir," Adam murmured deferentially as he came to a stop in front of Ted. All evidence of his anger had disappeared, and a teasing light danced in his eyes. "Will there be anything else, sir?" he added with exaggeratedly raised brows.

"Not at the moment," Ted replied seriously, joining in Adam's nonsense.

"Then do I have your permission to escort this maid onto yon dance floor?"

"Yes—begone." Ted waved his hand impatiently. "And let me get back to the business of seducing this lovely lady."

Adam's soft laughter covered Jen's small gasp of surprise. Expecting some caustic comment, Jen glanced at Liz. But although her cheeks flushed becomingly pink, Liz lowered her eyes and remained silent.

Shrugging off the cloak of obsequiousness, Adam grasped Jen's hand and pulled her with him as he started to walk away.

"Each to his own method," he drawled sardonically. "Have at it, the couch is all yours."

Ted's laughter followed them as they made their way to the dance floor. Their progress was slow as the room was crowded. Every table was occupied, and the throng at the bar was now three deep. And over all a holiday atmosphere prevailed.

The area designated for dancing was even more dimly lit than the rest of the large room. The faces of the couples, moving slowly to a ballad, were barely discernible.

As they stepped onto the dance floor Adam released her hand and slid his arms around her waist. After a moment's hesitation, Jen placed her hands on his shoulders, ignoring the amused expression that crossed his face at her reluctance to encircle his neck with her arms.

They had taken no more then a few steps when the record ended, and yet it had been enough time for Jen to pick up his style. His hands holding her firmly at the waist, Adam waited until the next record was dropped onto the turntable. When the raspy voice of Bob Seger, singing something about his lady, came from the speakers, Adam's hands moved up her sides to her shoulders, then along her arms to grasp her wrists and draw them up and around his neck.

Following his steps automatically, Jen felt a shiver zigzag down her spine as his hands retraced their route to her waist. Then the zigzagging shiver splintered and sent stabbing points of excitement all through her body as his hands drew her closer to him. At least two inches still separated them, yet she felt suddenly breathless. Why, she wondered muzzily, did this man have this effect on her? She had danced in exactly this manner many times before, with many different men, yet never had she felt quite like this.

Tall as she was, Adam was several inches taller, and almost afraid to look at him, Jen fastened her eyes on the rolled collar of his sweater. As the music and Seger's sexy voice swirled around and through her, Jen felt Adam lower his head a moment before his warm breath teased the skin at her temple.

"Be brave, Jennifer," he whispered invitingly, his hands moving slowly, caressingly over her back. "Take that one tiny step necessary to bring your body against mine."

Gasping as much from the shaft of near painful longing that shot through her as from his words, Jen lifted startled eyes to his and was suddenly lost in a world of hot brown velvet. Thought suspended, she moved closer, feeling her breath catch again as his arms tightened to mold her softness to the hard contours of his larger frame.

Jen no longer heard the music or was aware of the other dancers around them. Melting warmth seeping through her, she stared in bemused fascination as Adam slowly lowered his head even more. By the time his mouth touched hers, her lips were slightly parted in acceptance.

Adam's kiss was brief in duration and gently experimental in nature. When he lifted his head Jen felt acute disappointment and dissatisfaction. Her feelings left her mind numb with shock. She had not reached the age of twenty-three without being kissed, by several boys and, later, young men. But although she had enjoyed being kissed, she had quickly called a halt to all wandering hands and even the hint of the tip of a potentially probing tongue. Always before, the mere thought of an intimacy beyond a meeting of lips plunged her into a near panic. Yet now she felt perversely cheated by the lack of aggression from a man she did not know. The realization that she had wanted that aggression chilled her mind. Sensing her mental withdrawal, Adam tilted his head back, his eyes narrowing as he studied her pale cheeks.

"Is something wrong?" His tone was soft but rough-edged, and somehow Jen knew he was wondering if she had been offended or turned off by his kiss.

"No, no." She shook her head to add emphasis to her denial. "It's been a long day and I'm tired of dancing." It was a blatant lie. She wasn't in the least tired, merely confused by her out-of-character response to him, and in truth, she could have moved to the musical beat, within the circle of his arms, for hours.

"Okay, let's go see what kind of progress Ted is making in his seduction of Liz." While he was speaking he came to a stop at the edge of the dance floor nearest the bar. His eyes, steady on her face, lit with laughter at the pink tinge his words brought to her cheeks. "I've shocked you?" he asked softly.

Feeling her face grow warmer still, Jen slid her arms from around his neck and lowered them to her sides. Lowering her eyes at the same time, she wet her lips and murmured, "Yes, a little."

"Why?" His one hand left her waist and came up to catch her chin, gently lifting it until she was looking at him again. "Why does the idea of Ted seducing Liz shock you? He has been seducing her with his eyes all evening. Why should saying it out loud shock you?"

"But they hardly know each other," Jen blurted, suddenly nervous because she felt sure that although he used Ted and Liz's names he was talking about two other people, and she was one of those people. "They only met today."

"And a required amount of time must elapse for a man and woman to conclude they want to make love?" His tone was lightly teasing, but all the laughter was gone from his eyes. "Would you be less shocked if they waited until tomorrow?" he prodded gently. "Or should it take a week or a month or a year?"

Beginning to feel badgered, cornered, Jen stared at him in confusion. Why was he doing this? What had she said to cause the fine, underlying trace of sarcasm that had entered his tone? She had the uncomfortable sensation that she had disappointed him, and she didn't know why. Had she no right to feel a little shocked at the idea of Ted and Liz spending the night together when they'd only met that very morning? Had she no right to her own principles of moral behavior? Anger stirred and she stepped back and away from him.

"I'm sure my views on the subject will have very little bearing on its outcome." Though she managed to keep her tone soft, there was a chill to it that betrayed her anger. She spun away from him but was brought up short by his arm snaking around her waist.

"Where are you going?" The mild demand in Adam's voice irritated her, and she made no attempt to hide it.

"Why, back to Ted and Liz!" she exclaimed nastily. "I wouldn't want to keep you from satisfying your avid curiosity about the progress Ted's making."

Before she could move away from him, his fingers dug into her waist, and with a jerk of his arm he pulled her to him.

"Jennifer"—Adam's soft voice now held a hint of his own anger—"let's have one thing clear. I don't give a damn what Ted and Liz do. And I'm sure as hell not going to pass moral judgment."

"But I haven't—!" Jen began in astonishment.

"Haven't you?" he cut in roughly. As if suddenly realizing where they were he released her and said tersely, "I think we'd better go sit down."

With an angry toss of her fiery head Jen swung away from him. Head high, she made her way through the crowded room, bewildered by the deflated feeling his rebuke had caused. Why in the world should she be hurt by his opinion? Why should she care what he thought? If they could leave tomorrow, she would probably never see him again. Jen had to smother the moan of protest that thought generated.

Eager to escape her confusing thoughts and emotions, Jen smiled brightly at Ted and Liz as she came to a stop in front of them.

"What happened to your dancing partner?"

56

Ted's mild inquiry startled her. She had assumed Adam was right behind her.

"I—I don't know," she answered faintly, biting her lip in disgust at the tremulous sound of her voice. Her eyes searched the crowded room without success; there was no sign of him. Sinking into a low chair facing the sofa, Jen stared blankly at the braided rug on the floor, unaware of the look that passed between Ted and Liz, or the understanding smile that tugged at the corner of Ted's mouth. For a brief instant Jen's expression had been as transparent as glass and had revealed more to Ted of her feelings than she was as yet ready to admit to herself.

Had Adam been so angry at her he'd gone to his room without even bothering to say good night? But why take his anger out on Ted and Liz? She felt miserable, and suddenly very tired. *I may as well go to bed,* she thought dejectedly, *and leave Ted and Liz to get on with whatever they're going to get on with.*

"Lord, this is a thirsty crew."

Jen's head snapped up at the sound of Adam's quietly dry voice. One quick glance was enough to tell her he was either no longer angry or masking it perfectly. He was carrying another carafe of wine in one hand and a large pewter mug filled with ice cubes in the other.

"We were wondering what had happened to you." Ted, in the process of pouring a glass of wine for Jen, lifted the carafe Adam had brought earlier. "I'm glad you decided to brave the bar, though. As you can see, Liz and I have just about killed this. How did you know?"

"Elementary." Adam grinned, setting the wine and mug of ice on the table that separated the sofa from the chair Jen was sitting on. "Every red-blooded male knows the first move in seduction is to get the lady smashed."

"Good thinking." Ted grinned back at him, then laughed out loud at the color that rose in both Liz's and Jen's cheeks.

"Ted, stop it," Liz scolded gently. "You too, Adam,"

she tacked on as his soft laughter blended with Ted's. "You're embarrassing Jen."

Still laughing softly, Adam dropped to the floor as agilely as an Indian and sat, cross-legged, eyeing Jen wickedly. "Are we embarrassing you, Jennifer?"

Feeling her color deepen under his teasing gaze, Jen gratefully accepted the glass of wine Ted handed to her and took a sip before answering.

"Yes, a little." Although her cheeks were hot, Jen had somehow managed to keep her tone cool. "I've never heard anyone discuss seduction so casually before."

"Casual?" Adam's eyes pierced hers. "Believe me, I'm never casual about seduction."

Jen smothered her gasp inside her glass. She gulped the cool liquid, then nearly choked as Ted concurred.

"No man worth his salt is ever casual about seduction."

Something in Ted's tone made Jen look up questioningly.

"Don't tell me you haven't noticed what's happening here?"

"Happening here?" Jen repeated blankly. "I don't understand."

The motion of Adam's head drew her eyes. His expression was rueful as he shook his head. "Look around, Jennifer," he said exasperatedly. "I mean, really look."

Following the direction of his waving hand, Jen glanced around the room. During the last hour the festive din of conversation had dropped to a muted hum as couples sat at tables and at the bar, talking softly. At first the significance didn't register. She was on the point of asking someone to explain when the word *couples* flashed through her mind. There had been very few couples when she'd entered the room. Slowly, carefully, her eyes made another circuit of the room before returning to Adam.

"Talk about casual seduction," he murmured. "This place has an epidemic."

"You really have been missing it, Jen," Liz chimed in

softly. "It's like a chess game, every move well thought out and planned." Her pretty mouth curved wryly. "Most of them had never spoken to each other before they came in here tonight."

While Liz was speaking, Jen's shocked eyes watched Terry leave the bar arm in arm with a man. The man was Larry Gordon's complaining companion from the bus. Jen had to fight down the urge to run after Terry and tell her the man was engaged to be married. "What has come over everyone?"

"It's like a fever." Ted answered the question Jen hadn't even realized she'd asked aloud. "A fever that melts inhibitions. Caused by being snowbound."

CHAPTER 4

"But we've only been snowbound for a few hours!" Jen cried incredulously.

"Makes no difference," Ted said quietly, handing Adam a glass of wine before emptying the first carafe by topping off Liz's and his own glasses. "I've been driving these tour buses for over ten years, and it's been an education." He took a long swallow of his wine before continuing. "When away, even for short weekends, some people act completely different than when they're at home. And for some reason being snowbound makes them kick over any remaining traces of inhibition altogether. The first time I was snowbound my reaction was very similar to yours." He smiled gently at Jen. "I've learned a little about human nature since then."

"But—"

Jen's protest was interrupted by the arrival of a flushed, breathless Lisa. Jen was sure the young man with her had not been on the bus.

"Do you think we'll be going on to the lodge tomorrow, Liz?"

Jen frowned at the almost fearful note in Lisa's voice. Unless she had misinterpreted that note, Lisa was hoping Liz would say no. Yet Lisa had been eager to get to the lodge. Obviously the young man with her was the cause of her about-face. Liz's reply did little to relieve Lisa's anxious expression.

"I just don't know, Lisa."

"We'll have to wait until morning and see what condition the roads are in," Ted put in quietly.

"Okay," Lisa sighed. She started to turn away, then glanced at Jen. "Will—" Lisa hesitated before going on rapidly—"will you be going up to the room soon, Jen?"

Jen felt as if a spotlight had been turned on her, and she didn't like the feeling. That Lisa was hoping Jen would say no was as clear as if she had shouted it. *Dammit*, Jen thought irritably, *she's asking me to stay out of the room while they make use of it—and each other.* Disgusted anger warred with disbelief inside her mind. Cute, bubbly little Lisa, ready to jump into bed with a man she'd just met? And what about Terry? Had she gone to *his* room?

Jen had the uncomfortable feeling that by agreeing to stay where she was for a few more hours she'd be condoning the act. And she didn't condone it. On the other hand, she'd already been accused of making moral judgments once that night. What could she say? Adam made the decision for her.

˙ "Jennifer will be here, with me, for some time yet." Adam's face and tone were devoid of expression. "Did you want her for something?"

"No—no," Lisa said hurriedly. "I just wondered."

"Don't wander too far, little lady." Adam laughed. "You may get lost."

Lisa flashed him an interested, impish look before walking away.

Jen was furious, both with Adam for interfering and, strangely, with Lisa for the parting glance she'd thrown him.

"You see what we mean, Jen?" Liz smiled wryly.

"Yes, I see," Jen mumbled around the anger choking her. "I still don't understand, but I certainly do see."

"Don't worry about it," Ted advised softly.

"And take that guilty look off your face," Adam chided.

"What do you mean, guilty look?" Jen bristled. "Why should I look guilty? I haven't done anything wrong."

"That's right, you haven't," Adam retorted. "But for a second there you were actually considering going up to your room just to thwart Lisa's plans. That's why I took the initiative." The mild emphasis he'd placed on his last sentence made it clear to Jen that he was very much aware of her anger, and at least one of her reasons for it.

"But my not going up is almost like saying I approve," Jen argued. "And I don't. She doesn't even know him and—"

"It's none of your business," Adam cut in harshly. "That girl is over the age of consent. Who she gives that consent to is entirely up to her." He paused, then sighed. "For God's sake, Jennifer, this place is full of consenting adults, not little kids. And if I read the signs right, they're all very eager to consent to almost anything. If it offends you, don't look. Sit back, drink your wine, and ignore it. It can't possibly hurt you unless you become a part of it."

"A part of it!" she cried. "I think it's disgusting."

The moment the words were out, Jen wished she'd kept her mouth shut. How could she have forgotten Ted's teasing but nonetheless serious words about seducing Liz? Avoiding Adam's eyes, shifting uncomfortably, Jen watched the color drain out of Liz's face.

"Jennifer—" Adam began warningly.

"She's young, Adam," Ted interrupted imperturbably. "And she's entitled to her own opinion." Smothering a yawn behind his hand, he got to his feet. "I'm tired and I'm going to bed and"—he stretched his hand out to Liz—"regardless of anyone's opinion, I'm taking Liz with me."

Her eyes on Ted's, Liz rose, placed her hand in his, and after murmuring a soft "Good night," left the lounge area with him.

"That wasn't exactly tactful," Adam admonished quietly.

The fact that Adam voiced her own uneasy thoughts put Jen on the defensive.

"I'm sorry if my 'young' opinions annoy you," she flashed scathingly. "Please don't feel you have to wait with me until Lisa and her friend vacate the room." With a wave of her hand she sneered, "Go join the mature, consenting crowd."

Feeling like a complete fool yet stubbornly refusing to back down, Jen watched as the muscles in his legs tensed before, straight-backed, he rose smoothly to his feet. As he turned away from her she had to bite her lip to keep from crying out a plea for him to stay. Closing her eyes, she let her head drop back wearily against the chair. What had come over her? With a few ill-chosen words she had shattered the camaraderie the four of them had shared. At the sound of ice tinkling against glass she lifted her eyelids a fraction.

Adam hadn't gone at all! Peering at him through her lashes, she watched as he poured wine over the ice cubes he'd dropped into his glass. After lowering himself onto the sofa he stretched his legs out, crossed his ankles, then looked directly at her. His gaze was pensive and held a hint of sadness.

"Are you still mad at me?"

His quiet tone seemed shaded by the same sadness Jen was sure she'd seen in his eyes. With a pang Jen wondered if he too regretted the loss of warmth that had surrounded them.

"No." Jen's voice was husky with remorse.

"Then why don't you come sit over here"—he patted the cushion beside him—"and talk to me?"

Jen needed no further urging. Pausing to drop an ice cube in her now warm wine, she sat down beside him and drew her legs up under her body.

"I"—she hesitated, moistened her lips—"I'm sorry for flaring up like that, Adam. I wouldn't blame you if you did walk away from me."

Adam was almost reclining, his head resting on the low back of the sofa. As he turned his head to look at her he brought his hand up to her face and, with a feather-light touch, drew his long forefinger across her cheek and down her jawline.

"I'm never going to walk away from you, Jennifer."

Jen was unable to control the shiver his touch sent scurrying through her body, or the heat that followed at the low intensity of his voice. *What did he mean by never?* She asked the question of herself because she didn't have the courage to ask him. Gathering her scattered wits, she drew a long breath to calm her suddenly racing heartbeat. Then her breathing and heart seemed to stop altogether as Adam's hand curved around her nape and drew her head to his.

Sharp disappointment washed over her when, her lips a bare half inch from his, he turned his head slightly and bestowed a chaste kiss on her cheek.

"I want to kiss you, Jennifer." Adam's throaty murmur replaced the disappointment with an exciting chill. "But later, when our audience has thinned out a little." The movement of his lips as he spoke teased her skin. "For now, talk to me, tell me about yourself."

Releasing her, he slid slowly into a sitting position and fixed her with that warm velvet gaze. Straightening, Jen gripped her glass with trembling fingers and brought it to her lips for a quick sip. The dryness in her throat somewhat relieved, Jen drew her eyes away from his compelling stare.

"What do you want to know?" The question was directed at the crackling fire.

"Everything. Anything. Whatever you want to tell me," his quiet voice prompted her. "Most importantly—is there a man in your life?"

"There are several." Jen's eyes swung back to his. "None of them serious."

"Good." There was a wealth of satisfaction in that one word. His eyes caressed her face a moment before he added dryly, "I'd have hated the idea of cutting another

64

man out." Ignoring her soft gasp, he allowed a rough edge to tinge his tone. "I'd have hated it, but I'd have done it nonetheless."

"Do you think you could have?" Jen exclaimed, fighting the will-destroying pull of his eyes.

"I don't think so, I know so," he stated flatly. "You know it too."

Unable to deny his assertion, yet unable—or unwilling —to admit it, Jen again tore her eyes away from him. His soft, mocking laughter sent warm color flying into her cheeks.

"Am I going to have to drag every detail out of you?" Adam chided laughingly after she'd remained quiet for several moments. "Or did you want to play twenty questions?" Without waiting for her to answer, he sighed exaggeratedly. "Okay, question one: Where were you born?"

"Right outside Norristown," Jen said to the fire.

"Now, that wasn't hard, was it?" he teased. "When?"

"What?" Jen turned her puzzled face to him. "Do you want the month, day, and year?"

"Jennifer"—he heaved another long sigh—"I'm trying to find out how old you are. Give me a number."

"Twenty-three."

"Ah, now we're getting somewhere." Adam smiled. "Parents?"

"Two." Jen smiled back.

"Cute." His smile stretched into a grin. "Siblings?"

"One." She returned his grin, her eyes beginning to dance with devilry.

"Male, female? Single, married? Younger, older?"

"A sister," Jen laughed. "Older by three years. Married —with a twenty-year mortgage and a two-year-old son."

"Careful, there," he intoned. "You answered two questions I didn't ask."

"Sorry."

"You're forgiven." He waved his hand airily, and Jen's eyes fastened on his slender yet strong-looking wrist. As it had early that morning, the sight of that wrist, and the hand connected to it, sent a thrill through her midriff. Shifting her eyes, she found him watching her closely.

"See something you like?" His voice had dropped to a low murmur.

His tone caused her breathing to grow shallow. "Is—is that one of your twenty questions?"

"One of the most important ones." Adam's eyes followed the tip of her tongue as she wet suddenly parched lips. "Would you consider wetting my lips like that?"

Oh, Lord! Jen's lashes fluttered from the force of the anticipatory quiver that ran pell-mell over her skin. Suddenly too weak to break the hold his hot velvet eyes were imposing on her, she had the uncanny sensation that the electrical charge that had flashed between them from their first meeting had tautened and was drawing her slowly but inexorably toward him.

"Adam—"

Every tiny particle of moisture in her mouth and throat had been used up in her effort to articulate that softly moaned plea. Bemused, completely unaware of her action, her tongue again snaked out in an attempt to quench the fiery heat consuming her lips. Adam unwittingly broke the invisible cord pulling at her when his eyes dropped to her mouth.

The moment that had seemed to last an eternity was gone. Jen heard, and understood, Adam's harshly released sigh.

"God, I want to kiss you," he muttered raggedly. "I wish these would-be lovers would get on with it and coax their victims off to bed."

Jen felt a finger of ice pierce through her. Is that what *he* was? A would-be lover who just happened to need a little more privacy? And what about her? Was she an intended victim? No more, no less? A potentially willing female to be used as a bed warmer on a snow-filled night?

The thoughts chilled her, stiffening her spine until her head snapped up rigidly.

"Are you anxious for them to finish their plays so you can make one of your own?" Jen's voice sounded cold and distant even to her own ears.

"Dammit, Jennifer." Adam actually seemed to growl with exasperation. "Don't go all uptight and frigid on me again."

Although Jen tried to avoid his eyes, they caught and held hers. Hard anger had replaced the dark brown liquid warmth.

"If I had wanted to make that kind of play, I'd have made it long ago." His tone smacked at her as effectively as a palm against her cheek. "If all I wanted was a quick roll in the hay I could have had you in the sack hours ago."

His overwhelming confidence angered her while at the same time it had her wondering if she would have been able to withstand him had he made such a play. Her own self-doubt inspired the impetus to challenge him.

"You're that good, are you?" she sneered at him—and at her own uncertainty.

"I'm that good." His flat agreement, delivered without a hint of bravado, drew a shocked gasp from Jen. Before she could form the jumbled words of defensive ridicule that crowded into her mind, he added forcefully, "But my expertise—for want of a better word—has nothing to do with it. You have been mine for the taking from the moment we met. I know it, and although your mind's been dodging around in a frantic attempt to deny it, you know it too."

Damn him! Double damn him for making her face the fact that she had—as he so aptly phrased it—been dodging frantically. She didn't understand what was happening to her, and like everyone else, what she didn't understand frightened her. And, like some, being frightened called forth the urge to fight. Tossing back the fiery mane that exactly matched the color of the flames leaping in the fireplace, Jen forced a note of disdain into her voice.

"I won't even honor that claim with an argument. Now, if you'll excuse me?" Moving slowly, as if afraid she'd break if she moved too quickly, Jen carefully set her still half-full glass of wine on the table at the end of the sofa. "I'm going to bed—alone." Her final word was issued with hard bitterness.

"Stay where you are." Adam's hand, clamped firmly onto her shoulder, prevented her from rising. "That's better," he murmured with approval when she settled back without protest. "By the way," he began innocently, "what bed were you going to go to? Or"—Adam's tone remained innocent, but his eyes began to glitter devilishly —"were you thinking of joining little Lisa and her playmate? A sort of—ah—ménage à trois?"

"Adam, really!" Jen choked, outraged at the suggestion even though she knew he was teasing.

"Jennifer, really," he mocked sadly. "The laces binding you are very straight and exceedingly narrow."

"You consider me narrow-minded because I can't approve of indiscriminate sex?" she breathed in astonishment.

"It's not a question of approval or disapproval," Adam informed with a shake of his head. "It's a question of tolerance and understanding." He frowned at the look of distaste that crossed her face. "Will you tell me something, innocent one?" At her hesitant nod, he gibed, "Why the hell should you care who goes to bed with who?"

"Why?" Jen cried in disbelief. "Why, because it's positively indecent, that's why!"

"No kidding!" Adam marveled sardonically. "You consider Ted and Liz indecent, then?"

"Well—" Jen felt trapped by her own hasty words. A vision of the quietly competent Ted and the patient, likable Liz rose in her mind. In no possible way could she

68

truthfully label them indecent. "No—but—" Her moment's hesitation was all he needed.

"That's right, there are no buts. Ted and Liz are both very nice people." Adam paused, his hand sliding over her shoulder and down her arm to grasp hers tightly. "Why should the fact that they decided to advance their relationship from the social to the physical upset you? Good grief, don't you know the sex drive is the strongest of all?"

"Yes, of course," Jen snapped defensively. "But there is such a thing as pride and self-restraint."

"Bull," he snorted crudely. "At least in Ted and Liz's case. I recognized what was happening between them at once. Maybe because the exact same thing was happening to me." Lifting her hand he stole her breath completely by bringing her fingers to his lips, caressing them gently. "I want you." His warm breath feathered over her skin, setting off a delicious shiver that skipped up her arm. "I have wanted you since our eyes met, around Ted, at the bar. But I want more than one night. I want every night."

"Adam—I—" Jen swallowed painfully against the tightness in her throat, then blurted, "I can't go to b-bed with you tonight."

While she'd been stuttering her way through her refusal, Adam's tongue tasted the soft skin between her thumb and forefinger. As she finished speaking, his teeth nipped at the mound at the base of her thumb.

"Who asked you?"

"But—" Shocked at the sharp sense of rejection she felt, Jen had difficulty pushing words past her trembling lips. "I thought—you said—"

"I know what I said," Adam chided gently. "I also said I would not be satisfied with one night." He paused to lift his head and pin her with his eyes. "Jennifer, there is one thing I want you to remember always. And that is, unless I'm obviously teasing, I always mean what I say. And what I said was—I want every night."

Jen felt as if the flames in the fireplace had leaped from

their food of logs to dance over her skin. *He couldn't mean—!* But what was he thinking of? Could he possibly have a long-standing affair in mind? And if not, that *could* only mean—marriage?

Her mind reeling with her confused conjecturing, Jen glanced around the room, unaware of the dark brown eyes filled with compassionate understanding watching her; her eyes darted back and forth like an animal that had caught the scent of danger. It required several circuits of the room before the realization hit her: except for a few hangers-on at the bar, the place was now empty.

Finally, not knowing where else to look, her eyes reluctantly came back to Adam.

"I don't understand," she whispered tremulously. "What, exactly, *are* you saying?"

Releasing her hand he drew his legs up as he shifted his body to the edge of the sofa. Muscled forearms resting on his knees, he stared for long minutes into the slowly dying fire.

Tension coiling more tightly inside her with every dragging second, Jen found herself unable to tear her eyes from his sweater-clad broad back. When he did finally turn, it was so sudden that Jen jerked back against the sofa.

"I think you know *exactly* what I'm saying, Jennifer." His softly caressing voice reached out to encircle her with warmth. "But I also think it's too soon to put into *exact* words." His eyes left her to skim quickly over the room. When they came back they settled on her mouth. "Besides, my speech is never very exac* when my lips are otherwise occupied."

The anticipation rising in Jen suffered a minor setback when instead of moving closer to her he turned away.

"Adam?"

Leaning forward, he set his empty glass on the floor.

"I'm only getting rid of the glass, darling."

On first meeting she had wanted to hear that endearment on his lips, and the effect of it on her senses was more devastating than she could ever have imagined.

"I—I like the sound of that," Jen offered timidly.

"That's good." Shifting his body on the edge of the sofa, Adam turned back to her from the opposite direction. "I intend calling you darling a lot." His hands came up to caress her shoulders before encircling her neck. "I liked the way you just said 'Adam.' " "As he moved closer to her, his thumbs followed the line of her jaw. "It had a breathy, pleading sound. Very exciting." His head drew close to hers, and Jen's lids closed as her mouth opened. "Say it again, darling."

"Adam." Her voice was a mere sigh against his lips.

"That's even more exciting." The words were spoken on her lips, into her mouth.

His kiss began as gently as the one he'd given her on the dance floor, but within seconds his lips hardened with command and his chest crushed her breasts. As the kiss deepened, long fingers slid into her hair, the tips pressing against her scalp as if to urge her closer, closer.

Jen's mind was beginning to feel disconnected from her body when her mouth was suddenly released. Lifting his head, Adam's eyes fastened onto the backs of the last two customers at the bar. Untangling his fingers from her hair, he slid his hands back to her shoulders.

"I don't want to be interrupted," he murmured as his clasp on her shoulders tightened. "Or watched."

Moving her gently, he slid her down until she was lying flat on her back. Fingers sliding back into her now disordered mane, he slowly bent over her.

Cold with a mixture of excitement and nervousness, Jen, her breathing growing more and more shallow, watched as his face came closer. *What am I doing here?* she thought distractedly. *I shouldn't be here.* A strange, desperate fear gripped her and her eyes flew to his. It was a mistake. Like a small frantic animal caught in quicksand, Jen's eyes became caught in the hot molasses depths

71

of his. She didn't speak—she could not—but she didn't have to; Adam read the panic in her hazel eyes. Inches from her, his head dipped lower and his lips pressed to the wildly fluttering pulse in her neck.

"Don't be afraid, Jennifer." Adam's voice, muffled against her skin, had a soothing, hypnotic effect on her. Feeling as though everything inside was beginning to melt, Jen moaned softly as his lips left a trail of heat up her neck to the ticklish, tender skin behind her ear.

"But I am afraid, Adam." Jen's whisper had the sound of a very young girl. "I've never felt like this before and—and I don't understand what's happening to me."

"Don't you?" His murmured tone challenged her ignorance. "You've never wanted a man, physically, before?"

Jen's breathing was so constricted she could barely whisper, yet she had to answer, make him understand.

"No. Not like this, anyway. This—this frightens me, Adam."

"You are—" Adam paused while he lifted his head, his eyes searching her face—"you are still innocent?"

"Yes."

Jen's cheeks grew warm under his steady regard. Why did having to make that admission embarrass her? She knew the answer to that one, of course. How many times had she received pitying glances from young men she'd refused? And it wasn't just the men either. Although she was closed-mouthed about her personal life, her friends knew, somehow, that she'd never—in the words of one outspoken friend—"come across." That same friend had laughingly dubbed Jen "the citadel." And all her friends seemed to regard her with genuine sympathy.

Hadn't she heard of the liberated woman? Jen had been asked repeatedly. Didn't she know she had as much right to sexual freedom as any male? Wasn't she—for heaven's sake—frustrated? Jen had answered yes, yes, and no to those questions—always basically the same, if couched differently—so often that her responses had reached the point of automatic flatness.

Now, with Adam's eyes searching her face, Jen questioned herself. Why had her admission made her uncomfortable? Was she frustrated? And had that unrealized frustration been the cause of her strange and immediate reaction to Adam? Did she, subconsciously, long to, as Ted said, kick over the traces, cast off the shackles of her state of innocence?

Her thoughts made her even more uncomfortable and she moved her head restlessly. On making her murmured reply Jen had lowered her eyes, unable to face the derision she was sure Adam would not be able to hide. Now, after his long silence, she lifted her lids.

"Why are you blushing?" There was not a hint of pity or derision in his tone or expression. "And why did you look away from me?"

Something about his stillness told Jen that he already knew the answers but wanted vocal confirmation from her. And what would he do if she gave him that confirmation? Laugh? Deride? Jen knew she could not take that. Not from him.

"Let me sit up, Adam." What had been meant as an order slipped out as an agonized plea.

"No." No lack of firmness in his tone. "Answer me, Jennifer. Why should admitting to your virginity make you this flustered?"

"Don't you know?" Feeling trapped, Jen flung the words at him defensively. "Don't you know that in this bravest of brave new worlds, in this sexually enlightened generation, I'm an oddity? A museum piece? A holdover from the Victorian age?" Her spark of defiance died leaving her voice strained, shattered. "Don't you want to laugh or shake your head sadly and tell me I don't know what I'm missing?"

"No, I don't want to laugh or shake my head sadly." Adam's hands, grasping her head, forced her to look at him. "Actually I feel like shouting in sheer relief." A gentle smile curved his lips at her confused, wide-eyed stare. "What you've just said so bitterly is true. You don't know what you're missing, but I'm delighted you've missed it."

"Why?" Jen blurted nervously. "I thought—well, I've been told that men prefer a woman with some experience."

"I'm sure some do, and to be blunt, I've enjoyed my share, but—" Adam stopped speaking abruptly. Dipping his head swiftly, he caught her slightly parted lips with his. The feel of his tongue gliding along her lower lip drew a shuddering response from her. He pulled away at once.

"Did you like that?" he asked with almost clinical detachment.

Always before, the smallest foray of a male tongue had repelled her. Yet now she felt cheated by his withdrawal. If she was honest with herself as well as with him, there was only one answer she could give.

"Yes."

"That wasn't even the tip of the iceberg," Adam murmured softly. His fingertips gently massaged her scalp. "Jennifer, the world of the purely physical, the sensual, is a world apart. The only confines of that world lie within the individual imagination. It can range from a hurried, frantic, almost animalistic coupling to an exquisitely beautiful experience. I want to be the one to introduce you to that world." His mouth brushed hers gently. "You are my darling, and I want you." The uneven tremor of his tone sent an expectant shiver through Jen. "But I want more than mere willingness. I want even more than eagerness."

He paused to draw a ragged breath, affording Jen the opportunity to insert, more than a little fearfully, "Adam, I don't understand. What is it you want?"

"Exactly what I'm willing to give," he answered without hesitation. "Unconditional surrender."

74

Jen went stiff with apprehension. Did he mean now? This minute? But she couldn't, she thought frantically, she wasn't ready. His calming voice cut into her scuttling thoughts.

"Don't panic, Jennifer. I will not use force. I will not use coercion." A fleeting smile touched his firm lips. "I am not turned on by the idea of dragging you into that physical world. We will journey—together—or we will not journey at all." One dark eyebrow arched. "Will you go with me?"

"I—I—" How could she answer when she wasn't quite sure she even understood him?

"You may pause, or come to a complete stop, anywhere along the way, but"—his eyes bored into hers—"if you decide to embark on this venture with me, I expect your complete honesty."

"In what way?" Jen's voice was a shakily expelled whisper.

"If anything I do to you displeases or frightens you in any way, you must tell me." His voice grew husky, intimate. "By the same token, if I please you, you must let me know, either verbally or—or in any way that feels natural to you. Now do you understand?"

Closing her eyes against the hot velvet lure of his, Jen lay perfectly still. If this was a line—a new, refined way of making a proposition—it was a very effective one. For without knowing quite why, Jen trusted him implicitly. Still she hesitated.

"I may cry 'halt' at any time?" she asked softly.

"Yes." Adam didn't elaborate any further. He didn't have to. She believed him.

Taking him at his word she whispered, "When does this journey begin?"

"Now."

Jen felt the word like a wisp of silk ruffle her lips. Adam's mouth opened over hers invitingly. After a very brief hesitation Jen's lips parted to join with his.

There were no wildly ringing bells. No explosion of skyrockets. Unlike his kiss of a short time earlier, Adam's firm lips made no demand. Sweetly, gently, with a slowness that was, in its very languidness, exciting, Adam explored the outer edges of her mouth.

"Adam?" The pleasant, though uncertain, sound of Bill Wakefield's voice separated them. "Miss Lengle?"

"Right here, Bill." Releasing the cradling hold he had on her head, Adam straightened, placing a restraining hand on her shoulder when she made a move to sit up.

"I'm sorry to intrude," Bill said quickly, "but I wanted you to know that the bar's closing."

"And you'd like us to vacate the room?" Adam asked quietly.

"Not at all." Bill snorted. "Hell, I don't care if you stay in here all night. I just wanted to warn you that the lights in here will be turned off shortly, and to ask if you'll make sure the fire screen is in place before you leave."

"Will do, Bill."

"Okay, thanks. Good night."

Jen's soft voice blended with Adam's in wishing Bill a good night. A moment later his voice filtered through the empty room.

"Oh, by the way, it has started snowing again."

"Well," Jen murmured, "I guess that answers the question as to our going on to the lodge tomorrow."

Turning his head slowly, Adam stared down at her, his face free of expression.

"Does that disappoint you?"

Remembering his cautioning words about honesty, Jen shook her head.

"No." Then, with a teasing note she added, "I don't ski very well anyway."

"I'll teach you to ski," Adam offered as he lowered his head to hers. "Among other things," he added as his mouth touched hers.

This time he let the kiss deepen, his lips hardening on

76

hers when he felt her response. Caught suddenly in a maelstrom of new, exciting sensations, Jen curled her arms around his neck, her fingers digging into his hair. And now it was her fingers that pressed against his head urging him closer. She was breathless and trembling by the time his mouth left hers.

Moving leisurely, his lips explored her face before, trailing moist fire across her cheek, they found her ear. She gasped when his teeth nipped gently at her lobe, and she moaned softly when the tip of his tongue followed the outer ridge of her ear. And all the while his hands slid caressingly over the silky material of her blouse, warming the skin of her shoulders, her arms, her waist.

Her breasts seemed to fill achingly as his hands moved slowly over her midriff. When his hands cupped the expanded mounds, she shuddered with the intensity of pleasure that skittered madly through her entire body.

His hands were removed instantly and his breath tickled her ear as he softly questioned, "No?"

"Oh, yes." Jen's gasped reply was barely audible, as was her soft sigh as his hands returned to stroke her breasts. Turning her head, she kissed the corner of his mouth to draw his lips coaxingly to hers.

His mouth touched hers, retreated, touched again, over and over. First her lower lip was caught, caressed, inside his mouth, then her upper lip received the same loving attention. They were both breathing in short, ragged gasps when he pulled himself away. Turning from her, he slid off the edge of the sofa onto the floor.

"Cooling off period," Adam rasped tersely. "I think we'd better talk for a while."

CHAPTER 5

Talk? Talk!! God, she could hardly breathe. And even if she *could* breathe, the way her mind was whirling, she doubted her ability to put together a lucid sentence.

Drawing his legs up, Adam sat, forearms crossed over his knees, chin resting on his arms, staring broodingly into the fire. Sometime during those mind-shattering moments while she'd been lost inside the euphoria of Adam's mouth, the lights had been extinguished and she had not even noticed.

Now, as her breathing leveled off and her rioting emotions cooled to languor, Jen studied the flickering play of dying firelight across Adam's face. What she viewed increased her pulse rate again. His strong face, alternately cast in shadow and light, had suddenly become the most important countenance in the world for her. Was it really possible, she mused dreamily, to fall in love within the time span of twelve or so short hours?

Yesterday she'd have laughed at the idea of love at first sight. Love grew as two people got to know each other, and deepened with the passage of time—didn't it? Yet she could no longer deny, even to herself, that *something* had happened to her the moment their eyes met. No, something had stirred inside her at the sight of his hand hours before their eyes met. But could it have conceivably been the first pangs of love?

Jen didn't know and at the moment was simply too lethargic to delve into it too deeply. What she did know

78

was that merely looking at his shadowed profile sent the blood charging through her veins making her fingers ache with the need to touch him. Wiggling her body, she shifted to the edge of the sofa. Her movement broke through his concentration on the crackling logs.

"Talk, Jennifer." Adam sounded as shaken as she felt.

"What should I talk about?" Jen asked huskily, her eyes arrested by a small shallow indentation near the hairline at his temple. Before he could answer she murmured accusingly, "You should not have scratched."

"What?" He jerked around to stare at her, his back rigid with tension. "I scratched you?" His eyes moved swiftly over the exposed skin of her face and neck. "Where?"

"Not me," Jen corrected with a soft smile. Lifting her hand, she placed her fingertip on the tiny hollow. "You have a scar from scratching when you had chicken pox. How old were you?"

"Seven or so—I was in the second grade." His hand came up to cover hers, pressing it against the side of his face. Her palm felt the play of small muscles that tugged a smile from his lips. "Is it your turn to play twenty questions?"

"May I?" The tremor that ran down Jen's arm was revealed in her shaky voice. Hesitantly she moved her fingers to outline his eyebrow.

"Sure." Adam's hand moved with hers. "I want you to feel free to ask me anything." His long fingers slid along hers. "Touch me—anywhere."

"How old are you?" The words came out in a breathless rush.

"Thirty-two." Adam laughed softly.

Giving in to the urge to imprint his likeness on her fingers as well as her mind, Jen's fingers explored his forehead before moving on to trace his hairline.

"Where were you born?" she asked in bemusement as she drew a line from his hair to the bridge of his nose.

"Tokyo."

That caught her attention.

"You were born in Japan?"

"Yes." Adam's voice held a smile. "And spent the first ten years of my life there."

While she digested this bit of information, her fingers gently probed the soft hollow under his left eye. When his eyes closed she tested the texture of his eyelashes.

"You have very long lashes, you know that?"

The laughter that erupted from him momentarily dislodged her hand. The pressure of his fingers guiding hers away from his lids allowed him to open his eyes again. "Is that a note of envy I hear in your voice?" he asked around his laughter.

"Of course." Her soft laughter joined with his. "It isn't fair, you know. Do you have any idea what we females have to do to make our lashes look that long and full?"

"Life's cruel," he teased, drawing her hand down to cover his mouth.

"And you males don't apprecia—oh!" The tip of his tongue against her palm stole her breath. "I—I thought you wanted to talk," she gasped the moment she got it back.

"No, that isn't what I *want* to do." His hand moved away from hers. "But I think that is what we'd better do." When she lifted her hand from his face he muttered, "Put it back. I didn't say we couldn't touch while we talk."

As he was speaking he shifted position. Turning to her, he imprisoned her loosely by placing his left forearm on the sofa on her right side and his right hand near her head. During the shifting, her hand slipped from his face. Bending over her he repeated, "Put it back."

His hand moved in time with hers, and she felt his fingers touch her face at the same time hers touched his.

"Talk, Jennifer."

"I—you—" Jen had never realized the skin on her face was so sensitive. Yet it must be, for the feather-light touch of his fingers could be felt clear through to the bone.

Marshaling her dissolving senses she whispered, "You came to the States when you left Japan?"

"Yes, to Philadelphia," Adam whispered back, a smile twitching his lips.

Covering the betraying twitch with her fingertips, Jen sighed, "Do I amuse you?"

"You delight me." The smile grew under her fingers. "You excite me," he murmured. "Talk, Jennifer."

"Your father was in the service?" Fingertips moving slowly, she delicately outlined his mouth.

"No." His breath tickled her palm. "Not then anyway. He was stationed there at the end of World War Two, before I was born. He fell in love with the country and its culture. When he came home, back to Philly, he formed a partnership with my mother's brother, opened a small showroom, and went into the importing business. As soon as the business was established he packed up most of his belongings, my brother, who was then two years old, and my mother, who was pregnant with me, and went back to Japan. I was born three months after their arrival there."

Adam's hand had not been idle while he was speaking. Moving slowly, his fingers had examined her facial features, as hers had explored his earlier. At the same time his left hand had awakened every nerve ending in her right arm with slow, caressing strokes from her wrist to her shoulder.

"And he stayed ten years?" Jen's voice had grown husky with the tightness invading her chest and throat. The incongruity of their conversation and the aura of sensuality surrounding them was creating havoc with her senses—physical and common.

"No, he never came home." Being very careful not to tug painfully, Adam put both hands to work arranging her hair into a fiery aureole around her head. "My mother brought me home when I was ten." Dipping his head swiftly, he rested his face against hers and murmured, "You have very beautiful hair, Jennifer." Lifting his head

81

with obvious reluctance, he went on softly, "My father and brother remained in Japan. I've been back and forth like a swinging door since then."

"Your parents are divorced?" Jen stirred restlessly at the gaspy sound of her own voice. He was too close—much, much too close. Her movement brought his eyes to hers. A flame as bright as any in the fireplace blazed in their dark depths.

"No, they are not divorced."

"But—" Jen began, then paused, a frown betraying her confusion.

"Within the last twenty-five years they've seen each other approximately twenty-five times," Adam said quietly, steadily.

"But how can a marriage like that survive?" Jen asked in astonishment, visualizing the close, comfortable relationship her parents shared.

"Why shouldn't it?" Leaning back away from her, Adam shrugged. "They genuinely like and respect each other. How many couples do you know, married over thirty-five years, that can truthfully say they still have those feelings? Some quietly hate each other. Others are merely bored to numbness with each other. And that includes a lot of people married one hell of a lot less years. The only reason most of them stay together is their innate fear of change or being alone."

Jen felt chilled, both by his sudden withdrawal and the cool superiority of his tone. Perhaps that happened to some couples, but surely not the majority. Her own parents were proof of that. On the defensive, Jen plunged into the role of advocate for tradition.

"But without the day-to-day sharing, both of good and bad, there is no *real* marriage. There is no *real* communion, not only mentally but—" Jen broke off, the argument dying on her lips at the stonelike quality that had replaced the velvet warmth in Adam's eyes.

"Do you actually believe two people have to live togeth-

82

er, endless day in, endless day out, to share that communion?" Adam asked austerely. "Believe me, they do not. My parents have shared the *important* things, including my brother and me."

"But that was so unfair to you!" Jen cried indignantly.

"In what way?" Adam replied coldly, moving even farther away from her. Before she could speak he answered for her. "By not being subjected to the petty jealousies most parents indulge in? I can assure you neither my brother nor I feel deprived about that. We had the best of both and of each other."

In one smoothly executed movement he turned away from her, leaned forward to scoop up his glass, rose with feline grace to his feet and, walking to the table, asked softly, "Would you like more wine?"

His sudden action, his soft tone, following so swiftly after his taut stillness and his cold voice, left Jen feeling disoriented and confused. Moving with much less grace than he had exhibited, she sat up, murmuring a hesitant "Yes, please."

He filled the glasses and handed one to her, then stood watching her as he drank half the contents of his glass in a few deep swallows.

Jen withstood his penetrating gaze as long as she could before protesting softly, "Why are you angry with me?"

"I'm not angry, Jennifer," he denied with a brief shake of his head. Sighing softly, he refilled his glass again before dropping onto the sofa beside her. "What I feel is impatience. Over the years I've become accustomed to the questions concerning my parents' life-style but"—he shrugged—"from you those same questions generate impatience in me."

"But why?" Jen's widened eyes mirrored her deepening confusion. "I'm very much like other people."

"You've just answered your own question." Adam's smile held self-mockery. "If you're honest you will admit that from the moment we met, something—I don't know

83

what, but *something*—happened between us." His eyebrows rose, and she answered his silent query with a nod. "Yes," he said softly, "and I guess I expected too much." Adam shrugged again. "I don't even know what I did expect exactly." A wry smile curved his lips. "Automatic understanding plus a deep sense of simpatico, I suppose." The wry smile turned sad. "Very unrealistic, I know—but the hope was there."

"Adam—I—" Jen paused, groping for the words that would banish the sadness from his eyes. She didn't even understand why his obvious disappointment in her should hurt her so much, but it did. And so, making no attempt to hide the hurt, she said wistfully, "I'm sorry, but I am very much like other people. I had a very ordinary upbringing. I have never even heard of the kind of relationship you have described to me." She bit her lip, pleading, "Help me to understand."

Adam's eyes studied her broodingly for long seconds before, sighing deeply, he leaned to her and kissed her mouth very gently.

"I'm sorry, too," he murmured against her lips. "Okay," Adam said briskly as he sat up, "I'll make it as brief as possible. My parents *do* love each other. But they are both very independent people. My mother's a feature writer for a Philadelphia newspaper—has been since she graduated from college. She took a leave of absence when my brother, Luke, was born, and resigned when Dad decided to make the move to Japan. She worked for a while on a small English-language paper over there, but it didn't satisfy her." He paused to drink deeply from his glass before explaining, "She writes articles on vacation spots and places of interest on the East Coast. Places accessible, financially and timewise, to people limited to one or two weeks vacation."

"What is your mother's by-line?" Jen asked when he paused again to sip at his wine.

"Janet Elliot," Adam answered, one brow arching. "Have you read her articles?"

"I never miss them!" Jen exclaimed. "In fact it was because of an article she did on the ski lodge we were headed for that I decided to go on this tour."

Adam was nodding his head before she'd finished speaking. "I was headed for the same lodge." He laughed softly. "She is very good at what she does, and you can be sure if she claims a place is interesting, and worth the money, it will be. Anyway"—he shrugged—"as I said, she lasted ten years in Japan and then told my father she was going home, and back to work. Both Luke and I were present at that discussion. There were no accusations, no bitterness. If anything, my father seemed grateful for the ten years my mother had remained with him."

"Grateful?" It was impossible for Jen to hide her surprise and shock at that word.

"Yes, grateful." Adam's rough tone underlined the words darkly. "People can't own each other, Jennifer."

"I know that!" Jen exclaimed in protest. "But if there is real love between two people then surely—"

"Surely, what?" he interrupted harshly. "One should be willing to sacrifice all ambition, all personal dreams, to the other? Subjugate themselves at whatever cost?"

Wincing, Jen shrank back, away from his lashing tongue. The look on her face drove him to his feet. Breathing deeply, his back to her, he placed his now empty glass on the table, then stood as if collecting his thoughts, one hand absently rubbing the back of his neck. When he turned back to her it was so sudden Jen's body jerked.

"Dammit, Jennifer—" Adam stopped abruptly as his eyes caught the movement of her trembling hands. With an impatient grunt, he plucked the glass from her hand with a terse "Give me that before you spill it all over yourself."

Biting her lip, Jen watched him warily as he set her glass

85

beside his own. When he again turned to face her, all signs of his impatience were gone.

"How can I make you understand?" He sighed softly, shaking his head. "If they had remained together they would very probably hate each other today. As it is, they still genuinely love and respect each other."

"But you said they've only seen each other about twenty-five times in the last twenty-five years."

"That's right," Adam replied quietly. "So?"

"Well—?" Jen paused, searching for words, then she blurted baldly, "Adam, you reminded me earlier that the sex drive is the strongest of all. I don't see how—" Jen faltered, again searching for words.

"They have both had 'friends' over the years," Adam informed steadily.

"Friends?" Jen stared at him blankly a moment before, eyes widening, she asked faintly, "You don't mean—?"

"I mean exactly that," he inserted flatly.

"But—but that's—" Words failed her, and feeling her face begin to burn, she lowered her eyes.

"That's what?" Cradling her head with his hands, Adam forced her to look at him. "Immoral? Disgusting?" Bending over her, he stared directly into her eyes. "How do I make you understand?" he murmured. "I knew, and liked, every one of their 'friends.' There were only a few, on both sides. Their current friendships, or lovers, have been constant for several years now. My mother's 'friend' is a very prominent industrialist." His eyes grew soft, pensive. "My father's 'friend' is a gentle, exquisitely lovely young woman."

Jen was not so innocent or naive that she didn't know of the extramarital activities some people indulged in. But never had she heard of a situation quite like Adam had just explained to her. To Jen, it sounded cold-blooded and thoroughly selfish. In no way could she ever imagine herself loving one man while accepting another simply to appease the demands of the body. And she knew, without a shred of doubt, that the knowledge of the man she loved, and who supposedly loved her, performing that act of appeasement with another would be an unbearable reality she could not live with. Jen shook her head sharply in negation of the idea.

"I can't understand it, Adam," she whispered raggedly. "I don't even want to understand it. The thought that two people who claim to love each other could—" Jen's voice diminished to nothingness, and again she shook her head sharply inside the loose confines of Adam's hands.

Those hands, gentle till now, tightened, long fingers digging through her hair into her scalp. Holding her still, he grated, "I know it could not work for everyone. Ideally, each individual should be able to choose his own way, his own life-style. Females as well as male. But it usually comes down to one giving way to the other."

"But that's what marriage is all about, isn't it?" Jen cried. "The give and take of two individuals learning to live together?"

Why did she suddenly have the very uneasy feeling they were no longer talking about his parents? Jen wondered despairingly. And why did his opinion have the power to inflict the pain now clutching at her chest? She had no time to search for answers, for Adam, propping one knee on the cushion beside her, leaned very close to whisper harshly, "I should not have started this. I should have waited until we knew each other better." His digging fingers stilled a moment before beginning a sensuous massage down the back of her head. By the time his trance-inducing fingertips reached her sensitive nape, Jen was experiencing that all-over melting sensation again. Shivers skipping down her spine from quivering nerve endings, she was barely aware of Adam's words or the rueful tone of his voice.

"What I should have done is taken you to my room, bound you to me—at least physically—before attempting an explanation."

Jen's body grew rigid as the full context of his words registered on her bemused mind.

"No, you couldn't have." She moved her head restlessly from side to side in a useless effort to shake off his hands. "I would not have gone with you."

"Oh, Jennifer." Adam's voice had lowered to a caressing murmur. "Lie to yourself if you must, but don't try to lie to me. For while the words of denial whisper through your lips, the response of your body to my touch cancels them."

While he was speaking his hands moved as if to underscore his assertions. Trailing twin lines of fire, his fingertips followed the columns of her throat, paused a moment to explore her suddenly leaping pulse, then came together at the top button of her blouse. The small pearl button slipped neatly through the hole, and his fingers moved down to the next one in line, and then the next.

"Adam—stop—"

Adam's parted lips silenced her protest, his probing tongue crushed the meager remnants of her resistance. The pressure of his mouth on hers drove her head back against the soft cushion. The searching tip of his tongue drove all reasonable thought from her mind.

Although Jen was sitting down she had the oddest sensation of dropping through space. Reaching out blindly she grasped Adam's hips and hung on. Her mouth was released then caught again, teasingly this time.

While Adam's lips played games with hers, his hands slid inside her blouse and around her waist. The warmth of his palms sliding over the bare skin on her back drew a soft moan through her parted lips. The moan changed to a weak murmur of protest when his fingers deftly released the catch on her bra. Tearing her mouth from the drugging enticement of his, Jen gasped, "Adam, no!"

"I want to touch you." Adam's mouth moved along the curve of her neck to her shoulder with maddening slowness as his fingers examined her spine. His lips covered her shoulder, her collarbone, with moist, hungry kisses. "Touch you and taste you," he added huskily. "And I want you to do the same to me."

"No! Adam, I can't—" Jen's denial died as she realized the contradiction between her words and actions. As if she had no control over their movement her hands had slipped under and inside his sweater to his waist and were urging him closer.

His tongue probing gently at the hollow at the base of her throat, Adam lowered his body next to hers. Sliding his right hand around her rib cage, he drew a shudder from her by outlining the curve of her breast with his long finger. When, finally, his hand cupped the aching mound, Jen released a sigh that swiftly changed into a moan of surrender.

Beyond caring about the consequences, Jen tentatively stroked Adam's smooth, warm-skinned broad back. Feeling his muscles tauten and grow hard in response to her lightest touch shattered the last of her reserve, and she let her hands roam freely.

Head flung back, eyes closed, trembling in response to the breath-stopping sensation radiating through her entire body from the hardening bud Adam's fingers gently caressed, Jen whispered a soft protest when he lifted his mouth from her throat. The next instant the protest became a murmur of delight as his lips brushed hers.

"Lie with me, Jennifer." Adam's wine-scented breath feathered over her lips deliciously. "Now," he urged, "here on the sofa."

"Here!" Jen's eyes flew open, became enmeshed in the hot velvet depths of his. "Adam, there's a clerk at the desk in the lobby. What if he should walk in here?"

The flame that leaped in Adam's eyes brought full awareness of her own words, left no doubt of his own understanding. Although she had not actually said yes, her question had betrayed her compliance. What had become of all her strong moral standards? she wondered sickly, her eyes shifting guiltily from the bright flame in his.

"Adam—I—I—" Pausing to search for words of repudiation she really didn't want to speak, Jen ran her tongue over her dry lips.

"I asked you earlier if you'd consider wetting my lips like that," Adam whispered, bringing his mouth to within a breath of hers. "Will you do it now?"

"Adam, please—" Jen groaned.

"Do it," he ordered softly, touching his mouth to hers. His fingers, for the last few moments stilled into a firm cup over her breast, began a sense-heightening stroking motion.

Hesitantly, using the very tip, Jen slid her tongue along his lower lip. Adam's low groan of pleasure instilled a boldness Jen had never felt before. Extending the tip almost imperceptibly when she reached the corner of his mouth, she started the return trip. When she paused to outline the center dip in his upper lip, his mouth opened.

"Enter, darling," he urged hoarsely. "Explore, go crazy. Make me crazy too."

His mouth crushed hers, forcing her lips wide. Slowly, with much trepidation, Jen slipped her tongue into the moist warmth of his mouth, then, growing brave, joined into a game of tag with his.

Without knowing quite how he had done it, Jen found herself flat on her back again, Adam's hard chest pushing her into the sofa's soft seat cushions. Giving in to demands and urgings from deep inside, she dug her nails convulsively into his back.

The following minutes were the wildest Jen had ever experienced. Adam's mouth, opening wider, consumed hers, filling her with desire, while his thrusting tongue drove her to acts she'd never contemplated.

Arching her back, she pressed her throbbing breasts against his possessive hands while her hands tugged at his sweater to bare his chest.

"Oh, God."

The harsh groan sounded as if it were torn from deep within his throat as Adam tore his mouth from hers. His sudden withdrawal chilled and frightened her.

"What's wrong?" Jen cried in confusion. "Adam, don't you want me?"

Adam was on his feet, moving away from her. The tremulous note of fear in her voice stopped him in mid-stride. Swinging around, he came back to her, the expression of astonishment on his face answering her question before he opened his mouth.

"Not want you?" He laughed harshly. "Jennifer, I've got a hunger for you growing in me that will very likely take fifty years to appease." Bending over her, he grasped her shoulders and sat her up. Then, sitting beside her, he turned her so he was facing her back. His touch now coolly impersonal, he reached around her and expertly adjusted the lacy bra over her breasts before fastening the hook in back.

"Adam?"

"Shush, Jennifer." Lifting her hair to one side, Adam bestowed a tender kiss on the nape of her neck, then ordered softly, "Turn around, darling."

Obeying silently, Jen shifted around. Eyes lowered, she sat meekly while he buttoned her blouse.

"Look at me, Jennifer." His softly coaxing voice drew her eyes, shimmering with the threat of tears, to his. Now that her inflamed senses had cooled, sharp pangs of shame jabbed at her conscience, and as if that wasn't discomfiting enough, a deep feeling of rejection was poking holes in her confidence. The threat became the reality when two tears escaped to roll slowly down her cheeks.

Taking her face gently into his hands, Adam drew her to him with a murmured "Oh, my beautiful darling, don't cry. I want you so very badly but not here, not on this sofa. When I finally make love to you I want everything perfect for both of us." His mouth touched her lips as tenderly as it had touched her nape moments before. Then rising, he drew her to her feet.

"It's very late. Time for you to be in bed." Lifting his hand to her face, he wiped the tears from her cheeks, whispering, "Come, darling."

CHAPTER 6

The voices of Lisa and Terry, deliberately hushed so as not to disturb her, brought Jen half awake. The gentle click of the closing door as the two girls left the room imposed full consciousness.

Still sleepy, Jen pulled the covers up under her chin and, snuggling down, prepared to go back to sleep. The memory of Adam's parting words to her the night before sent her eyelids up.

"I think it's fairly obvious that no one is going anywhere tomorrow." Adam had murmured the words in between short, tender good-night kisses. "So sleep late, but when you do finally surface, search me out before you go to eat. I'll wait for you, and we'll have breakfast together." Nearly asleep on her feet, Jen had nodded her agreement and gave herself fully to his last, lingering kiss.

Now, all thoughts of sleep forgotten, Jen tossed the covers back and slipped off the bed, her hand groping for her watch on the shelf that separated the room's two beds. A quick glance at the watch told her it was 9:05. It had been after four when she'd fallen into bed, yet surprisingly she felt completely rested.

After a hasty jump-in, jump-out-again shower, Jen stepped into brief panties, black corduroy jeans, and her high boots. Opting for freedom of movement, she decided to go braless and tugged a heavy, cream-colored, long-sleeved velour shirt over her head. Swiftly but carefully, she applied a light daytime makeup, ending with a shimmering pink lip gloss, then with impatient strokes brushed her unruly red mop into some semblance of order. A final few seconds were used to adjust a fine gold chain around her neck, and she was ready to leave the room.

At the bottom of the curving staircase Jen paused to glance out through the glass entrance doors. The view that greeted her eyes was starkly white, but it had stopped snowing and a weak, watery light was fighting its way through the remaining pall of dirty gray clouds.

Except for the clerk at the desk—a young woman this morning—the lobby was deserted. The combined hum of voices and activity from the direction of the dining room indicated that quite a few of the motel guests were up and about.

Standing before the swinging doors into the room, Jen moved her eyes slowly from table to table. Although she saw several of her fellow bus passengers, including Terry and Lisa, there was no sign of Ted and Liz, or of the only one she really wanted to see—Adam.

Sighing softly, she backed away from the archway and almost into Bill Wakefield. Bill's staying hand on her arm stopped her retreat and prevented a collision.

"Good morning, Miss Lengle," Bill said, smiling brightly.

"Good morning." Jen returned his smile, hesitated a second, then glancing around, asked, "You haven't seen Mr. Banner this morning, have you?"

"Adam?" Bill's smile deepened. "Sure. He's out in the parking lot digging out his car."

"Oh!" Spinning around, Jen headed for the stairs. "Thanks, Mr. Wakefield." Flashing a wide grin, she ran up the stairs. Within minutes she came running back down again, wearing the bright red jacket with the hot pink stripes, a white knit cap, and matching mittens. At the bottom of the stairs she came to a full stop, soft laughter shaking her shoulders. Bill Wakefield, grinning broadly, stood waiting for her at the entrance doors, leaning on a large snow shovel.

"I thought you might want to give him a hand," he chuckled.

"If I can find him out there," Jen laughed as she walked to him.

"Oh, he'll be easy enough to spot once you get around that bus." He nodded his head at the large vehicle that blocked their view of the parking lot. "I've had men out there over an hour."

"Has there been any news on the road conditions?" Jen asked, taking the handle he held out to her.

"The road crews have been out since it stopped snowing around dawn. They were out last night but had to pack it in when it started snowing again." Bill shrugged. "The wind was blowing the roads closed as fast as they could clear them."

"Frustrating," Jen murmured. "Well, I'm no help to Adam standing here. See you later, Mr. Wakefield"—she indicated the shovel—"and thanks."

As Bill had promised, Jen had no difficulty locating Adam after she walked around the bus. The gold Formula, now cleared of its white cover, gleamed dully in the watery sunlight. Beside it, wielding his shovel with smooth precision, Adam was making noticeable inroads into the snow around his car. And Adam's labors were not the only ones showing results.

With surprised eyes Jen surveyed the cleared area around her. Off to her left a man in a Jeep with a snowplow attached to the front was making steady progress in clearing the parking lot.

Toting the shovel, Jen walked to Adam and, without saying a word, set to work. As she straightened to dump her first shovelful of snow, an arm snaked around her waist.

"Good morning." Adam's quietly caressing tone sent a

tremor down Jen's back. "You didn't sleep very long. Did you sleep well?"

"Yes." Turning inside the circle of his arm, Jen glanced up at him, feeling her breath catch at the warmth in his eyes. "Did you?"

"Not very." A rueful smile curved his lips. "I kept waking up, wishing you were with me."

"Oh, Adam. I'm—"

Adam's mouth, covering hers, silenced her. His lips were cold but every bit as exciting as the night before, and Jen responded eagerly. Adam began to deepen the kiss, then pulled back sharply.

"We're not going to get the job done this way." His eyes gleamed teasingly. "Even though I wouldn't be surprised if the snow is melting around my feet." Dipping his head, he stole another quick kiss before asking, "Have you had breakfast?"

"No," Jen exclaimed softly. "You said we'd have breakfast together."

"And we will," Adam chided at her reproachful look. "If and when we get the car dug out." Removing his arm, he stepped back. "So get to work, woman, I'm hungry."

Working silently, Jen matched Adam's pace until the area around the car was completely cleared of the heavy snow.

"I'm going to move the car closer to the entrance." Handing Jen his shovel, Adam slid behind the wheel and started the engine. "Go on ahead, I don't want to take the risk of having the thing slide around and slam into you."

Carrying a shovel in each hand, Jen walked to the front of the building, wincing at the stiffness in her back muscles caused by her unusual activity.

Adam carefully maneuvered the car into the part of the lot scraped clean by the snowplow, then joined her at the entrance doors. Relieving her of the shovels, he propped them beside the doors.

"We'll leave these handy for anyone else who might want to dig out. Now, let's go have breakfast."

After shedding jackets, caps, and gloves, and hanging them on a coatrack just inside the dining room, they made their way to the same table they had sat at the night before. They were no sooner seated when Adam lifted his arm to wave beckoningly to someone. Curious, Jen turned, then smiled a welcome to a very sleepy-looking Liz and a very satisfied-looking Ted.

"You two just crawl out too?" Ted drawled as he seated himself after seating Liz.

Jen felt her cheeks flush pink at the clear implication in Ted's question. He was assuming that, in the natural order of events, she and Adam had spent the night together in the same manner he and Liz had. Not bothering to disabuse Ted, Adam chided him disdainfully.

"I'll have you know, Jennifer and I have been industriously employed for the last hour"—a little exaggeration there, Jen thought—"digging my car out of fourteen inches or so of snow."

"I humbly beg your pardon," Ted apologized dryly. "Who do you have to know to get a cup of coffee around here?"

At that moment, as if on cue, the same young waiter who had served them the night before came up to the table carrying a glass pot of coffee and four menus.

"Good morning," he chirped brightly. "Four coffees?"

As the table was preset with napkins, flatware, and inverted cups on saucers, the waiter had only to turn the cups over and fill them at their chorus of assent. After doing so he passed out the menus and promised, "I'll be back in a few minutes for your order."

Liz slowly came awake as they ate their breakfast, and by the time the waiter refilled their coffee cups she had joined in with the light banter. The meal finished, Ted indicated a third refill of their cups as the waiter cleared the table, and then, after passing a pack of cigarettes around—which Jen and Liz declined and Adam accepted —he held the flame of his lighter to Adam's, lit his own, and said smilingly, "Now I feel almost human. What do you think our chances are of getting out of here today, Adam?"

"Nil," Adam replied flatly. "The road crews are hard at it, but I doubt if we'll be able to go anywhere before tomorrow morning."

Liz frowned, then glanced questioningly at Ted. "I guess we may as well head for home, then."

"I'm afraid so." Ted shrugged. "I'll see what I can find out as to road conditions upstate, but I doubt they'll be any better than around here."

"Probably worse," Adam inserted.

"If we have to go home, we're going to have a very unhappy group of passengers," Liz sighed.

"We have no control over the weather, Liz," Ted soothed. Then deliberately changing the subject he asked, "What do you do for a living, Adam?"

"I work for the oil industry." He named a large company. "Out of the Philadelphia office. I'm a sort of trouble-shooter."

Ted's eyebrows rose. "I'd have thought you a little young for that."

"Not really," Adam answered easily. "But the fact that I speak several languages, including Arabic, doesn't hurt."

That sent three pairs of eyebrows up, and Jen exclaimed, "Several languages? How many?"

"Japanese, Spanish, and Russian fairly fluently," Adam said. "And a smattering of Greek and Portuguese—plus the Arabic."

"You studied languages in school?" Ted inquired.

"The Russian and Spanish, yes, through high school and college. As I spent half of my formative years in Japan, I picked up the Japanese as a matter of course." At the baffled expressions that had been growing on Ted and Liz's faces Adam explained briefly. "My parents are scparated. My father lives in Japan, and I spent six months of the year with him while I was growing up. Also, as my father is in the export-import business, dealing mainly in Asian art objects, he made numerous buying trips to the Middle East. He always took me with him. At times those trips took up most of my six months stay with him and on several occasions included side excursions to Greece and Portugal." On noting the look of amazement on all three of the faces turned to him, Adam grinned. "Sounds like a very erratic way to grow up, I know, but at the time I thought it was perfectly normal." The grin widened. "I enjoyed every minute of it."

"I guess!" Liz exclaimed. "By comparison, my life seems very sheltered and awfully dull. I've never been any further away from home than Florida."

Liz had put Jen's own thoughts into words, except she hadn't even been as far as Florida.

"I was all the way to Virginia Beach once," she commented dryly. "How about you, Ted?"

"I've seen pretty much all of this country in the ten years I've been driving tour buses," Ted replied blandly. Then he added grimly. "After Vietnam I had no urge to ever leave this country again."

The very grimness of his tone cast a momentary quiet over the table.

"Sorry about that, guys." Ted grinned in apology. "I'm going to go and see what I can find out about the road conditions." Pushing back his chair, he smothered a yawn with his hand as he stood up. "Then, as I had very little sleep last night, I'm going to take a nap." He leered exaggeratedly at Liz. "Want to go with me?"

Although she blushed beet-red, Liz's "Yes" was prompt and clear. As she stood up Liz glanced from Jen to Adam. "What are you two going to do?"

Adam's quiet, serious "We're going to go play in the snow" drew surprised looks from both girls and a low chuckle from Ted.

"Each to his own games." Ted laughed and, grasping Liz's hand, he strolled away.

Finishing the last of her coffee, Jen studied Adam over the rim of her cup, a crawly sensation tickling the back of her neck. She *had* been longing to go romp in the snow, but how had he known?

"You do want to go out"—Adam's eyes as well as his tone teased her—"don't you?"

"Will you help me make a snowman?" Jen teased back.

"I haven't had much experience in the *man*-making line," Adam said, smiling wickedly, "but I'll do my best."

"You always made snowladies?" Jen fluttered her lashes over innocently widened eyes.

"Well, ladies, at any rate." Adam's soft laughter did strange things to Jen's breathing, while at the same time his words, though teasing, sent a tiny shaft of pain through her chest.

Why should you care? she chided herself as she preceded him out of the dining room. *Why should his none-too-subtle way of telling you he had made ladies bother you one way or the other?* A sharp memory of the melting feeling his mouth and hands had induced was all the answer she needed. Suddenly Jen hated the thought of any other lady knowing the feel of his mouth, his hands. *I'm jealous!* she thought in wonder. *I've known the man less than one full day, and I'm jealous of every other woman he has ever looked at with interest.*

Surreptitiously watching as he donned his outdoor gear, Jen acknowledged her feelings for what they were. *I'm in love with him. I barely know him and I'm in love. It's crazy. This doesn't happen in real life, does it? It's the situation,* she argued silently with her emotions. The snow. The proximity. Her eyes ran hungrily over his athletic frame, lingered longingly on his strong facial features.

Fighting the urge to reach out and touch him, she zippered her jacket with trembling fingers. The feeling of possessiveness that gripped her made a mockery of her inner arguments. All her previous beliefs went by the board. Whether it was supposed to happen "in real life" or not hardly mattered. She did love him, and the very thought of being separated from him now was unendurable.

In a somewhat shaken and unsteady state, Jen followed as Adam blazed a trail through the virgin snow around the one side of the motel building. The large, even expanse of pure white was a blatant invitation, and shrugging off the unfamiliar depression that had settled on her mind, Jen scooped up a handful of snow and tossed it at Adam.

Adam retaliated in kind, and that started a snow battle that soon had Jen shrieking with laughter and mock fear. The snowman was forgotten as the battle raged, wet and furious, for over an hour.

Stumbling away from Adam's too accurately aimed missiles, Jen came to a gently sloping bank near the rear of the motel.

"Oh, Adam, look!" Jen cried delightedly, staring at the bank. "A perfect place for angels in the snow."

"A perfect place for what?" Coming to stand beside her, Adam glanced at the bank then into her face in puzzlement.

"Angels in the snow," Jen repeated. "Haven't you ever made angels in the snow?"

"No." Adam shook his head. "How do you do that?"

"Give me your hand and I'll show you," Jen laughed up at him.

Ignoring the skeptical expression that crossed his face, Jen grasped the hand he held out and carefully lowered herself backward onto the smooth white bank. After extending her arms against the snow on either side of her body, Jen flopped them up and down while at the same time moving her legs in a scissoring motion. Then, jumping lightly to her feet, she turned to study the impression she'd made in the snow.

"Now, doesn't that look like an angel?" Jen indicated

the effect of head, wings, and full skirt her movements had impressed into the snow.

"Surprisingly it does," Adam admitted. Lifting his hands he caught the pointed ends of her upturned collar and drew her face close to his. "But I like my angels with a little more substance"—his cold lips touched hers—"and red hair"—the now warm lips trailed across her cold cheek—"and skin that's delicious even when it's been in the deep freeze."

"I'm no angel!" Jen exclaimed breathlessly.

"Any woman that has remained untouched until the age of twenty-three is either an angel or frigid," Adam laughed softly. "And after your response last night I think we can discount frigid."

"Adam, about last night"—Jen had a sudden, overwhelming need to explain her actions—"I've—I've never been like that with a man before."

"Do you think I don't know that?" Curling her collar more tightly, he pulled her against his taut body. His lips moved with shivering slowness from her temple to her jaw. "Lift your head—I want to bite your neck." The order was whispered in a reasonably good impression of every actor's idea of Dracula.

With a breathless, shaky laugh, Jen flung back her head and exposed her throat to his mouth. The touch of his lips was the trigger that sent her arms around his waist.

Locked together, indifferent to the cold, damp bite in the air, they clung: Adam to her collar, Jen to his jacket. The sudden movement of Adam jerking his head up and back startled a soft "Oh" from Jen.

"Your shirt collar is soaking wet," he growled softly. "You have got to be chilled to the bone. Why didn't you tell me?"

Without waiting for, or even allowing, her to answer, he released her collar and, clamping his arm around her shoulders, started toward the motel. As they approached the side of the building, an unmarked door opened and a motel employee struggled out with two large plastic trash bags.

Increasing his stride, Adam called, "Hold the door, please," then grinned a "Thank you" as they edged by the overstuffed bags. Within seconds they were standing outside the door to Adam's room. He inserted the key, then paused to gaze broodingly into her face.

"Okay?" he asked quietly.

Jen's hesitation was of a very brief duration, yet inside those fleeting seconds she became positive of two things. First, if she said "Yes" she would be agreeing to a total commitment, at least of a physical nature. Second, if she said "No," he would not insist but merely withdraw the key and escort her to her own room.

Without delving into her reasons, Jen gazed directly into his eyes and answered clearly, "Yes."

The door swung open, and Jen stepped into the room with an outward calm she was far from feeling. She had never been inside a man's room before. Excitement, coiling inside like an insidious reptile, vied with fluttering nervousness.

The room was a smaller replica of the one she shared with Lisa and Terry on the floor above, except there was only one bed—a double. Jen stared at the bed as if she'd never seen one before. The sound of the lock being set on the door sent a quiver of uneasiness zigzagging through her body. The sound of Adam's voice, for all its cool practicality, dried up all the moisture in her mouth.

"You'd better get out of those wet clothes."

They were standing just inside the door, and following his example, Jen pulled off her sodden mittens and cap.

"Just drop them where you stand," he directed quietly. "We'll collect them when we're dry."

Like a well-trained soldier she obeyed without question, her mittens and cap falling to the floor from nerveless fingers. Her jacket followed a moment later, and bending over, her trembling fingers went into battle with the wet zippers on the sides of her boots. By the time that tug-of-war ended, Adam had scooped up the wet garments and was busy draping them over the back of the room's lone chair.

"If you'll bring me the boots," he requested softly, "I'll sit them in front of the register." With a wave of his hand, he indicated the long, narrow heating vent in the far wall below the wide window.

Jen carried the boots to him, then stood staring out the window while he lined them up along the wall. The window looked out of the rear of the motel, but the magnificence of the snow-covered, mountainous terrain was lost on Jen's unseeing eyes. Gazing in at the riot of conflicting emotions pulling in different directions, Jen blinked, startled when Adam's fingers, examining her collar, brushed her neck. Although impersonal, the physical contact made her shiver.

"You can't stay in these wet clothes," Adam stated flatly. "I think you'd better have a hot shower."

"A—a shower?"

Up until this point Jen had not spoken, nor had she looked directly at him. Now, hearing the faint, tremulous sound of her own voice and hating the timidity of it, she looked into his face—and melted. His eyes had that warm velvet glow, and a tender, understanding smile curved his lips. The hand at her collar slid around her neck, his fingers gently massaging the tension-tight muscles.

"There is no reason for you to be afraid, Jennifer," he said softly. "I will ask no more of you than you're willing to give." Bending his head, he touched her mouth very lightly with his. "Now, go have a shower while I dig out something for you to wear." Turning her to face the bathroom, he gave her a gentle push, adding, "Then I'm going for a drink. What would you like?"

Pausing in midstride, Jen asked the bathroom door, "Could I have a cup of tea?"

"Jennifer" –Adam's beguiling voice coaxed her head

around—"you may have anything that is within my power to give you." His eyes caressed her face with a touch she could actually feel before, turning away abruptly, he chided, "Now, go jump under a hot shower. I'll hand something in to you before I go for our drinks."

The "something" he handed through the six-inch crack she'd made between door and frame at his knock was a long-sleeved tailored shirt in a silky brown-and-white pin-striped material.

After a prolonged shower that went a long way in soothing her frayed nerves as well as chasing her body chill, Jen procrastinated further by cleaning her teeth with a dab of Adam's toothpaste on the tip of her finger and giving her unruly hair a vigorous brushing with his tortoiseshell-backed hairbrush.

Although she grimaced with distaste, she stepped back into her lacy bikini panties before sliding her arms into the silky sleeves of his shirt. The garment covered more of her than her short nighties, the front and back tails almost touching her knees.

She had fastened every button on the shirt when, lifting her head, she caught her reflection in the mirror and was gripped by silent laughter. *Some siren you are,* she ridiculed her image. Scrubbed clean of makeup, the sprinkling of freckles across her nose stood out on her shiny face. Added to that, the demurely buttoned shirt gave her a very young, very virginal look.

What in the world could a man who had been all over the world and had probably known—and made love to?— some very beautiful women want with you? she derided her reflection. The thought—more of the other women than her own innocent appearance—sent a fierce surge of competitiveness through her. *Something* about her had attracted him—he had admitted that—and right now he was waiting for her on the other side of the bathroom door. Was she going to go to him looking like a mature woman or a sacrificial lamb? With steady fingers she opened the top buttons to a point between her breasts, then raised her hands to her head and deliberately tousled her hair. Moving her shoulders sensuously against the silky material, Jen threw a final, defiant glance at her image, then turned and walked calmly out of the room.

Adam had thrown back the bedspread and covers and was stretched out on the bed. His eyes were closed, his head resting on his arms. A cup of tea and an empty glass sat on the small nightstand beside the bed. Opening his eyes, he stared at her expressionlessly before nodding at the stand.

"You'd better drink your tea," he murmured tonelessly. "While *it* still has some warmth." On the last word his eyes closed again.

Sitting down on the very edge of the bed, her back to him, Jen reached for the cup blindly, wondering if his words held a double meaning, and he was trying to tell her his warmth had dissipated. She gulped thirstily of the tepid brew, emptying the cup in a few deep swallows. After replacing the cup on the saucer she clasped her hands together on her lap and raked her mind for something to say. His still-toneless voice ended her fruitless search.

"Do you want to go to your own room, Jennifer?"

"No!" Jen blurted without thinking. Swinging around to face him, she rushed on tremulously, "Do you want me to?"

With the same gracefully fluid movement he'd displayed the night before, Adam sat up and gazed squarely into her eyes.

"You know the answer to that question," he grated softly. Circling her neck with one hand, he drew her face close to his. "Are you afraid, Jennifer?"

"Yes, a—a little," Jen finally managed to answer honestly.

"But you still want to stay with me?" Adam asked with low urgency.

His caressing fingers at her nape set off a tiny explosion that sent a spear of flame down her spine. The very closeness of his mouth brought a sudden dryness to her own.

"Yes," Jen whispered hoarsely and heard the hiss of his indrawn breath as her tongue slid over her parched lips.

"Do that to me," he groaned an instant before his mouth covered hers. As if to coax her own, the tip of his tongue teased the barrier of her closed lips until slowly, hesitantly, she parted her lips and let the tip of hers meet his.

The shudder that Jen felt ripple through Adam's body instilled confidence, and lifting her hands to clasp his head, she parted her lips still more as she urged him closer. Her small advance was rewarded by a full-scale attack on her senses.

His lips hardening with mounting passion, Adam's mouth plundered hers hungrily. His hands, sliding sensuously over her silky shirt, found, then swiftly opened, the four buttons she'd left closed.

Barely breathing, Jen waited for the touch of his hands on her bare skin. When he pulled away from her, her eyes opened wide in confusion.

"Adam—what—?" The anxious protest died on her lips as she watched him tug his sweater over his head. The sweater went flying through the air, but Jen didn't see where it landed, for, as though drawn by a powerful magnet, her eyes clung to the naked expanse of his shoulders and chest. Her eyes continued to cling when he slid off the end of the bed.

With a boldness she had never before known, Jen watched as Adam flipped open the snap on his jeans, lowered the zipper, and watching her watch him, deftly shucked out of them. The very brief shorts that covered his loins left little to her imagination. Desire, hot and demanding, surged through her, and lifting her arms to him she whispered, "Adam."

107

Dropping back onto the bed beside her, he hauled her into his arms.

"Don't be afraid," he whispered against her lips. "I'll be as gentle as possible with you."

His kiss began very gently, but at her eager response his mouth crushed hers and his tongue plunged with the swiftness of a rapier, tearing at the fabric of her natural reserve.

Her inhibitions melting under the warmth of his caressing hands stroking her skin, Jen sent her own hands exploring. The feel of his hair-roughened chest, the way his back muscles tautened against her palms, blurred all rational thought.

His arms tightened, flattening her breasts against his hard body, and Jen felt herself falling with him as he dropped back on the mattress. His mouth moved on hers, searching, devouring, like a starving man offered a banquet. His hands moved restlessly under the shirt until they found her hips. Grasping her tightly, he shifted her over his flat stomach until she was lying between his thighs. The evidence of his growing desire for her fanned the flame his mouth had lit into a consuming blaze.

When his lips left hers to forage hungrily down the side of her neck, she gasped his name over and over again. Jen felt his muscles bunch an instant before he rolled her over and their positions were reversed.

Sliding his hard, sinewy body along hers, his lips ignited small fires from her throat to her quivering concave belly, while his fingers teased her nipples into pebble-hard arousal.

He brought his mouth back to hers to play, to tease, to torment, and to whisper words that shocked at the same time they excited and turned the flame in the lower part of her body into a hard knot of aching need.

As if he sensed the ripe fullness of that need, Adam quickly removed her panties and his shorts. Moving between her legs, he grasped her hips and probed carefully at her maidenhead with his manhood.

"Adam! Adam, it hurts!" Jen silenced her hoarse cry by digging her teeth into her lips.

Adam's body stilled. "I know," he whispered, bending close to her. His lips touching hers, he grated, "Take hold of me and hang on." At his last word his mouth covered hers, and the swift thrust of his body drew blood.

Under his caressing hands the pain and fear that gripped her dissolved, then re-formed into a driving urge toward fulfillment. When it came Jen cried out with the shuddering relief and, for a fleeting moment, teetered on the brink of unconsciousness.

The ragged sound of Adam's breathing drew her from the brink to awareness. His face was buried in her neck, and she could hear the rapid hammer beat of his heart against her chest. Lifting her hand from his back, Jen smoothed the sweat-damp hair from his forehead.

"Am I heavy?" he murmured against her throat.

"Yes." Jen's whisper held a smile. "A little. But it's a nice heavy."

She could feel his laughter rumble through his chest an instant before it touched her ears. Rolling off her, he sat up and pulled the covers up over them. Sliding his arms around her he drew her tightly against his body with a teasing threat. "You'd better have a nap and rest up; I'm not through with you yet."

CHAPTER 7

A hand nudging her shoulder shook Jen out of her seem-
ingly drugged sleep.

"Up and at it, sleepyhead," Lisa chirped when Jen
forced her eyelids to half-mast. "Liz has just informed
everyone that we're leaving in as close to an hour as
possible."

"An hour!" Jen's eyes flew wide open as she jerked into
a sitting position. Adam! The thought of him caused a
tightness in her chest. She had to see him! Shaking her
head to clear the sleep-induced fuzziness, Jen focused her
eyes on Lisa's grinning face. "But why?" Jen cried, jumping out of the bed. "What's the hurry? Are we going on
to the lodge? What time is it anyway?"

Lisa stood patiently throughout Jen's bombardment of
questions. When she'd finally run down, Lisa answered
slowly and concisely. "We are leaving in an hour because,
apparently, Ted has decreed it. And no, we are not going
on to the lodge. The hurry, according to Liz, is Ted's; he
wants to get us all home safe and sound." Lisa held up her
hand when Jen opened her mouth to protest. "It seems
Ted heard a weather forecast this morning calling for
more snow by late this afternoon. That set the match to
his fuse, and he sent Liz to roust us out. Liz assured me
he was not fooling around. He wants to get going as soon
as possible." Lisa turned away, then tossed over her shoulder, "Oh, yes, it's now"—a quick glance at her watch—
"nine thirty-five."

Jen stood blankly irresolute for several seconds. Adam. This time the thought of him galvanized her into action. Her need for haste overriding her innate neatness, she tossed her clothes carelessly into her suitcase, leaving out the things she'd need to get ready to leave.

After a quick sluice-down shower she pulled on underwear, jeans, a sweater, and the now stiff suede boots. Making do with a light makeup of tinted moisturizer and clear lip gloss, she then tugged her hairbrush impatiently—thus painfully—through her tangled red mop. Blinking against the tears that sprang to her eyes from the self-inflicted punishment to her scalp, Jen's fingers went to her naked throat and a small, soft smile curved her shiny lips.

Turning from the mirror, she tossed her brush and makeup pouch into the white case and locked it. Glancing at her watch, she nodded with satisfaction. The entire procedure of preparing to leave had taken her exactly thirty-two minutes, for it was now seven minutes after ten.

Having had a head start in their own packing, Lisa and Terry had left the room fifteen minutes earlier, Terry grumbling, "Ted or no Ted, I am not getting on that bus without at least a glass of juice and a cup of coffee to fortify me."

Now, her handbag slung over her shoulder, jacket over her arm, mittens and cap in one hand and her case in the other, Jen, moving as swiftly as her incumbrances would allow, left the room without a backward glance.

After dropping her suitcase to one side of the entrance doors beside the cluster of others belonging to the tour passengers, Jen headed for the dining room. Feeling as though it was becoming a habit, she peered over the swinging doors, her eyes honing in on the table in the far corner. Although Ted and Liz were there, there was no sign of Adam.

Sighing softly, Jen turned away. Was he still sleeping? It had been very late last night—or, more correctly, very early this morning—before he'd given in to the need for rest.

Deciding he *was* still sleeping, Jen walked purposefully to the reception desk. The clerk behind the counter was one Jen had not seen before.

"May I help you, miss?" he asked politely when she came to a stop at the desk.

"Yes, I—" Jen hesitated, then, her voice stronger, she went on, "I wonder if you'd know if Mr. Banner is still in his room."

"Mr. Banner checked out of the motel early this morning." The clerk's quiet reply held firm conviction.

"Checked out?" Jen exclaimed. Hearing the shocked tone of her voice, Jen swallowed against the sudden tightness of her throat telling herself there had to be a mistake. Much more calmly, she put her thought into words.

"I'm sure you're mistaken. I'm referring to Mr. Adam Banner, in room one-twenty-seven."

"No mistake, miss," the clerk returned politely. "I accepted his room key myself. He left just after six this morning."

Stunned, not even remembering to thank the man, Jen turned away, took three steps, then stopped to stare ahead blankly, seeing nothing. On the edge of her numbed consciousness she knew that soon, very soon, the pain would start, but for these few seconds, a shocked nothingness encased her in unfeeling stillness.

"Miss Lengle. Miss Lengle?"

The concerned edge to Bill Wakefield's tone finally penetrated. Reluctantly emerging from her anesthetized state, Jen blinked against the strained, gritty feeling in her eyes and turned with a vague "Yes?"

"Are you all right?" The concern was sharply evident now. "You're white as the snow outside."

"I'm"—Jen moistened her lips—"I'm fine." At his disbelieving frown, she added with a forced, ragged laugh, "I—I didn't have enough sleep and I'm not quite alive yet."

112

"I see." Bill's tone indicated he accepted her explanation with reservations. "I have a note for you from Adam." His eyes still narrowed on her pale face, he held a plain white envelope out to her.

"When—when did he give this to you?" Jen croaked as she took the missive from him.

"This morning, just before he left," Bill answered quietly. Then, more sharply, he asked, "Are you sure you're all right?"

"Yes, of course, I'll—" she began, then, catching sight of Ted and Liz, along with at least a dozen people from the tour, emerge from the dining room, she improvised, "I'll go have a quick cup of coffee to wake myself up." The envelope clutched in her hand, Jen made a beeline for the swinging doors.

After sitting down at a small table for two in a corner of the room that was nearly deserted, Jen tore open the envelope with shaking hands and withdrew the single sheet of motel writing paper. The note was written in a broad, neat hand, and the name Adam was slashed across the bottom. Teeth digging painfully into her lower lip, Jen read the words he'd left for her.

> *Jennifer,* (Jen could almost hear the caressing sound of her name whispering through his lips)
>
> *I've received an emergency call that leaves me no choice but to go home at once.*
>
> *I want so badly to talk to you and explain, but there is so little time, and I don't have the heart to wake you, knowing you have been in bed such a short amount of time.*
>
> *Why did you go?*
> *I'll ask that question again when I see you.*
> *I must go.*
> *I will call you.*
>
> *Adam*

113

An emergency call. I'll see you. I'll call you. The words stabbed in Jen's mind and heart like a blade heated red-hot. *An emergency call. I'll see you. I'll call you.* But would he?

Her teeth punishing her lip, Jen faced the possibility that she may have just read the lines of a classic brush-off.

No! The voice of reason denied that possibility. A similarly worded note from a man like Larry Gordon would have left no doubt of a brush-off. *But not from Adam.* Adam was the exact opposite of the Larry Gordons of the world. Wasn't he?

Fighting tears and a demoralizing sense of rejection, Jen hung on to the phrase *But not from Adam* through a glass of juice, the subsequent trip through the lobby, and right past the two people stationed at the entrance doors.

"Jen?"

The sharp sound of Liz's voice shattered the protective shell of concentration Jen had drawn around herself. Unaware that her face had a shockingly fragile look, or that her eyes betrayed her fear, Jen twisted her lips into a grim smile.

"Good morning Liz, Ted," Jen greeted the couple in what she hoped was a carefree tone. Their facial expressions left little doubt that she'd failed.

"What's wrong, honey?"

Sudden tears, fiercely hot, filled Jen's eyes at Ted's tone; he sounded so much like her father. Her poor excuse for a smile faded as she blinked back the tears.

"It's something to do with Adam, isn't it?" Ted went on softly.

"He's gone," Jen whispered starkly. "He left around six this morning." Swallowing convulsively, Jen looked around distractedly. "He left a note but—Ted, I'm afraid I've been a fool—" Her words trailed off as her voice became caught in the thickness of her throat. Moving jerkily, she put her hand out to push open the large door. A firm hand on her arm stopped her erratic motion.

"Jen, wait!" Though still soft, Ted's tone held enough of a command to halt Jen's flight. "I feel positive there's a good reason for Adam's sudden departure. He's not the type to—"

"How can you know?" Jen interrupted wildly. "How could any of us really know what type he is?"

Liz's softly gasped "Jen!" brought realization of the shrillness of her voice. Breathing deeply in an effort to control the surge of emotion over reason, Jen went on more quietly, "Maybe our judgment was clouded by what you yourself called 'snow fever,' Ted."

"I don't believe that, honey," Ted disagreed sternly. "I think you're too levelheaded to be caught up in something like that, and I've been in too many similar situations to get carried away with it."

And yet you latched onto Liz as quickly—no, more quickly—than that stranger latched onto Lisa, Jen argued silently. Aloud she murmured tiredly, "I want very much to believe that, Ted, but I—I have this fear that maybe Adam strung a line and I, very accommodatingly, swallowed the bait." Glancing up at him, she managed a weak smile. "I trusted him completely, and right now I'm trying to hang on to that trust. Please don't look so worried, Ted. Misplaced trust or not, I assure you I'll live."

Within the few steps required to reach the bus Jen somehow managed to compose her features into an expressionless mask. Smiling and nodding at the several greetings called out to her, she made her way along the bus's narrow aisle to the seat she'd occupied previously.

"You look like you're either still half asleep or stoned, and even knowing you such a short time, I'm sure it's the first and not the second."

Jen smiled bleakly at Lisa's teasing quip and nodded briefly at a crumpled-looking, sleeping Terry.

"It must be contagious. Terry looks completely out of it."

"Dance lag," Lisa laughed softly. "I practically had to drag her off the dance floor at four thirty this morning."

Four thirty! A wave of despair washed over Jen at the sudden memory of where she'd been at exactly four thirty. Dropping her handbag, cap, and mittens onto the aisle seat, Jen slid into the empty seat next to the window with a muffled, "I'm about ready to join her in dreamland. Wake me when the bus pulls into Barton's parking lot."

Lisa's soft chuckle and easy "Gotcha" relieved Jen's concern that her hint that she didn't want to be bothered during the return trip had not been received as an insult.

After making herself as comfortable as possible in the limited space, Jen shifted her mental gear into neutral and closed her eyes, determined to sleep and not think. She was only partially successful. Drifting in and out of a doze, she heard the bus door close; heard the murmur of conversation as Liz moved slowly down the aisle counting heads; felt Liz's presence and ensuing perusal when she paused briefly at the empty seat beside Jen. The last thing she was aware of was the lumbering motion of the large vehicle when Ted drove off the lot.

"What time is it?"

Terry's question, issued around a yawn, wakened her. Eyes closed, Jen waited for Lisa's reply. It came softly.

"Twelve fifty-one exactly, and we've been on the road for about two hours." Lisa's tone held a rueful note. "I sure hope we stop to eat soon. The toast and coffee I had for breakfast lost its power about an hour ago."

Jen grimaced at the mention of food and hunched her shoulders inside her jacket. At that moment she was positive she'd never want to eat again. Nevertheless, when Ted maneuvered the bus into the parking lot of a large restaurant some half hour later, Jen duly filed out with everyone else. This time they were not expected and the word was do your own thing, but please, do it within an hour.

Sitting in a booth with Ted and Liz, Jen pointedly avoided the subject of one Adam Banner. Shooting her worried glances but following her lead, they made a desultory attempt at conversation.

"Are we going to see anything of each other after we get home, Jen?" Liz asked somewhat hesitantly.

"Yes, of course," Jen answered quickly. "Call me some Saturday and we'll have lunch."

The look that crossed Liz's face, the way her fingers clutched the saltshaker she'd been toying with, made Jen realize how hollow and insincere her reply had sounded. Talk about classic brush-offs.

"I mean it, Liz," Jen insisted warmly, "I seldom work on Saturday, and then only in the morning. I could meet you for lunch somewhere, and then we could spend the afternoon shopping."

"And if I'm free, and you let me know in advance," Ted inserted, "I'll meet you later and take you both out for dinner."

Jen had to work at not letting her surprise show, for she had been sure that Ted and Liz had been indulging in a weekend fling. Hadn't Ted mentioned that he lived out near Harrisburg? Rigidly controlling her disbelief, Jen teased, "I never turn down an invitation for a free meal."

Surprisingly, Jen found her appetite restored with her first bite of the char-broiled cheeseburger the waitress placed in front of her. After polishing off the sandwich and the side order of french fries that came with it, she pushed her plate aside and drew her second cup of tea forward with a sigh of repletion.

"*Now* you look like you might live," Ted commented wryly. "When you sat down you looked like you'd been boiled, starched, and hung out to dry."

Jen obligingly gave him the smile he'd so obviously been angling for. With a nod of satisfaction Ted ushered them out of the restaurant and back onto the bus.

Jen's smile disappeared after she'd once again settled her long frame into the narrow seat.

"Going back to sleep, Jen?" Lisa inquired as Jen depressed the button that tilted the seat back.

"If I can," Jen replied softly, hopefully.

This time it didn't work. The numbing blankness of sleep, or even drowsiness, eluded her. Instead of lulling, the low murmur of conversation from the seat behind her tugged at her attention. Unwittingly she was cast in the role of eavesdropper.

"Believe it or not, he didn't lay a hand on me," Terry informed Lisa. "All we did was talk. That guy is so in love with his fiancée, he doesn't know which way is up. And I got the impression, more from what he didn't say than from what he did, that that sweet thing is leading him around like a trained poodle." Even though Jen mentally gave Larry Gordon's frustrated friend a pat on the back for decent behavior, she felt the same disgust for his fiancée that laced Terry's tone. For several seconds, as she mused on the stupidity of that sweet thing, the talk from behind swirled over her head, vaguely heard but not registering until a statement from Lisa made itself felt.

"Yes, I went to bed with him." The boldly, if softly spoken words jolted through Jen like an electric shock. But there was an even bigger shock to come, for Lisa continued in a dreamy tone, "And he's serious, I mean really serious. We're talking marriage-city."

Lisa's lightly flippant tone did not hide the underlying excitement and happiness bubbling beneath the surface. Jen's lids closed against the sting that attacked her eyes. As Lisa went on blithely, Jen's hands gripped the seat's armrest in silent protest.

"Keith's a salesman, and he lives out near Pittsburg. He has to finish the sales route swing he is on now, but he's coming to Norristown to see me before he goes home."

God, the same routine, Jen thought sickly. Songs and dances and fancy repartee, only in this instance, the words

118

to the song were changed to fit the situation. Jen could almost hear the man's oh-so-very-sincere voice. I've got to finish my route, baby, but I'll come to you as soon as I can.

Jen moved her head restlessly against the seat back. She didn't want to hear Lisa's story. It was much too similar to her own and, spoken aloud, sounded much too improbable, too brief encounterish.

"And you believed him? Oh, Lisa, that has got to be the oldest line going!" Terry exclaimed softly.

"Sez you," Lisa returned smugly. "And, yes, I believe him. Not only because I want to, but because he has proven himself to me."

"In what way?" Terry's skeptical question echoed the one in Jen's mind.

"By speaking to my parents when I called them to let them know I was safe," Lisa replied loftily. "He introduced himself to my father and mother in turn, accepted an invitation to dinner next Sunday, and then, after hanging up, he called his own parents and introduced me to them. And as if that was not enough proof, he asked his mother to call mine and assure her of his sterling character." Her soft, delighted laughter rippled raggedly along Jen's rigid spine. "But there's still more. He gave me, as a token, his class ring that—as you can see—I'm wearing on a piece of string around my neck."

Jen was electrified. Without her awareness, her hand released the armrest and moved to the base of her throat to begin a fruitless search. On Thursday night she had labeled Lisa a fool. In her arrogance, and from her citadel of virginity, she had made moral judgments on just about everyone. And then, less than twenty-four hours later, she had—Jen shifted uncomfortably as the word "eagerly" slithered into her mind—broken her own moral code. So maybe, she mused, in one form or another, we are all fools.

The motion of her fingers crawling agitatedly around her neck brought realization of their action—and the object of their search. With the realization came memories—sweet, painful, and a little bitter.

She had been awakened the previous afternoon by erotic tremors rippling through her body. The source of those tremors was the teasing play of Adam's lips. Moving with infinite slowness, his mouth explored the upper part of her back, inch by minute inch.

Still half asleep, Jen's body had moved sensuously in time with the rippling tremors. Her squirming had alerted Adam to her wakefulness. He had murmured something she didn't understand before brushing her hair aside to expose her neck. Now, a shiver feathered her nape at the memory of the sensations the touch of Adam's mouth against her skin had generated. So vivid was the memory, so intense the feelings inside her body, Jen lost all sense of time and place. She was no longer cramped into a narrow seat on a bus full of people. In the grip of memory she was warm and comfortable, curled lazily against Adam's smooth, hard body, his desire-husky voice barely reaching her ear.

"Do you like that?" Adam's warm breath, fluttering over the supersensitive skin at her nape, drew an involuntary moan from her throat. "Does it do funny little things to you?"

"Yes," Jen gasped softly on a quickly expelled breath.

"And this?" The warm, breathy flutter, the excitingly moist touch of his lips, moved down her spine.

"Oh, yes." Jen's gasp had a choking sound now.

"And this?" Adam's tongue, feeling to Jen like a hot, licking flame, drew circles in the hollow at the base of her spine.

"Ooooh—God, Adam!!"

Jen began to feel slightly delirious as Adam's mouth and tongue climbed back up her spine. By the time he turned her to face him she had the uncanny sensation of floating inches off the bed.

"This time there will be no pain." Adam's teeth nipped

playfully at her lower lip inbetween teasing kisses. "From now on it's sweet pleasure for both of us."

The truth in his promise was soon borne out. Jen had had no inkling of the varied and exquisite pleasure the act of making love could give. And the most delightful thing was that not only was the pleasure derived from Adam making love to *her,* the pleasure she derived from making love to *him* was every bit as wild, if not more so.

The tremors that awakened her the second time were of an altogether different kind. Jen knew it was late because most of the light had gone from the day. Except for the tepid tea, she had had nothing to eat or drink since breakfast. And the tremors rippling through her midsection were caused by her stomach's growling demand for food.

Slowly, carefully, she pushed back the covers. As she moved to sit up, Adam's arm curled around her waist, holding her still.

"Where are you going?" His voice was low, sleep-fuzzy.

"To my room," Jen answered softly, simply.

"Why?" Fully awake now, Adam's tone had grown an edge.

"Because I'm hungry," Jen laughed. Turning inside the circle of his arm, she leaned to him to kiss the side of his jaw. "And because I want to have a shower and get dressed." Having decided she liked the taste of him, she trailed her lips to his chin. The low growl her action drew from his throat gave her a feeling of power that enabled her to add, boldly, "And since it's your fault I missed lunch, I'm going to let you pay for my dinner."

"Really?" Adam's soft drawl was a delight to Jen's ears. "And here I had convinced myself that since I had brought some mild diversion to an otherwise dull afternoon"—he paused to nip gently at her lobe—"you would insist on repaying me by picking up the dinner check."

"Adam Banner!"

Rich male laughter followed her shocked exclamation.

Pulling her tightly to him, Adam kissed her breathless before bothering to reply.

"You-rang?"

"Your ears will ring from my blows if you ever again even hint that I would pay for—"

"You mean it wasn't worth the price of a dinner?" Adam interrupted in mock astonishment.

"Let me up this instant, you devil." Jen's command had very little force, issued as it was against his lips.

"A perfect match," Adam declared contentedly. "A devil and an angel." His mouth crushed hers for long moments, and Jen was beginning to have that floating sensation when he lifted his head to whisper, "I'd better let you go, my snow angel, or you'll be lucky to get out of here tomorrow morning for breakfast."

Jen sighed blissfully as she stood under the hot, revitalizing shower spray twenty minutes later. She was in love, and it was every bit as wonderful as she had hoped it would be. She felt fantastically good. Adam was perfect. The motel was perfect. The snow was perfect. Even she herself was perfect, if a little silly at the moment. Laughing aloud she shut off the spray and stepped out of the tub. As she patted at the rivulets glistening on her skin, Jen suddenly realized she was tinglingly aware of herself as a woman.

Standing on tiptoes, she examined as much of herself as possible in the small bathroom mirror. *Not bad, I suppose,* Jen thought, her eyes noting in detail the upper part of her torso. A little lanky, maybe. Lips pursed, she cocked her head, her glance resting on her breasts. At least they are reasonably full, she mused, and high. Wide-eyed, she watched a rosy-hued stain creep up her neck and mount her cheeks as the echo of Adam's whispered, "Your breasts are beautiful, Jennifer. They fit my cupped hands exactly, and make my lips hungry for more" came back to her tauntingly.

The very depth of her response to his hands, his lips,

and above all, to his body, had been a shocking revelation to Jen. She had gloried in his all encompassing touch and, in turn, had reveled in the feel of him against her own hands and lips and body.

The heat stinging her cheeks, the tingling in the hardening tips of her breasts, and the leg-weakening tightness in her thighs startled Jen out of her erotic reverie.

"You are a bona fide diz," Jen chided her reflection softly. "And if you are not very, very careful, that very, very sexy guy is going to wrap you up and stick you in his pocket." Somehow the soft admonition had the opposite effect than the one desired, for the girl in the mirror grinned expectantly and begged, "When? When?"

The door to a room a short distance down the hall closed as Jen, finally composed and dressed to vanquish, left her room. Her emergence was greeted by a low, appreciative male whistle. Glancing up, Jen's smile changed to a frown of consternation. Larry Gordon ambled toward her, his hot-looking eyes insolently stripping her of the soft, clingy, spaghetti-strapped dress she'd moments before slipped into.

"You look good enough to eat," Larry praised unoriginally.

Not by you! Jen thought waspishly. Aloud she managed a tight "Thank you, Larry."

Coming to a stop beside her, he turned to face her, one hand reaching out to grasp her arm.

"Have dinner with me."

Jen's back stiffened at the command—for it had been a command.

"No, thank you, I—"

"C'mon, honey, loosen up a little," Larry cajoled in a tone Jen felt sure was calculated to melt the heart of the most frigid of maidens. "We'll have a good dinner, a few drinks, a couple of slow and easy dances and then"—he paused to grin boyishly—"we'll really have some fun."

Yech! Jen was hard put to keep the rude noise to herself.

This creep, she thought scathingly, obviously believed he was Robert Redford, Adonis, and Lord Byron all rolled into one irresistible entity.

"Larry," Jen began patiently, "I don't want to have dinner, or drinks, or dances or"—his grasp tightening on her arm snapped her patience—"or anything else. Now, take your hand off my arm," she finished icily.

"What's wrong with you anyway?" Rather then loosening, his grip tightened still more. "You hide out all day like some kind of recluse, you don't join in on the fun. I know, because I've asked, that you've barely spoken to any of the men on the tour. Are you made of ice, for chrissake?" His mouth twisted nastily. "Or do you like girls?"

Jen's outraged gasp was drowned by the deceptively pleasant voice that floated down the hall to them.

"I told you once to back off, Gordon."

Two heads, Jen's and Larry's, swung to face the source of that voice. Although Larry's fingers relaxed their punishing grip, he did not at once remove his hold.

"I'm not going to say it again." Adam's voice lowered as he drew near them—lowered and roughened. Jen had to suppress a shudder of fear when she got a clear look at his face. Larry's reaction must have been very like her own, for at that moment his hand slipped limply from her arm. Adam's face was set into frighteningly harsh lines that warned of icy rage and his eyes glittered chillingly from behind narrowed lids. His voice, so in contrast with his usually mellow, pleasant tone was terrifying.

"Get lost, lover-boy," Adam dismissed Larry softly as he came to a stop next to Jen. "And if you touch her again I'll rearrange all your pretty white teeth."

Larry needed no further urging. Without a word he took off down the hall like a scalded cat. The moment he was gone, Adam slid his hand around her neck and pulled her against his chest.

"Are you all right, Jennifer?" The transition from

menacing to tender was so sudden it threw Jen off balance and she sobbed, "Oh, Adam, I was so frightened."

"Did he hurt you in some way?" Stepping back, away from her, he swept his eyes over her. It was too much.

"Oh, Adam"—Jen couldn't stop the laughter that gurgled from her throat—"*he* didn't frighten me. *You* did."

"I did!" Adam nearly shouted. "How?"

"You looked so—so deadly." Jen covered her mouth with her fingers to contain her laughter, but she couldn't cover the brightness in her laughing eyes. "You—you scared the hell out of me."

Adam looked at her disdainfully, but the corner of his mouth twitched suspiciously. "I think you're getting light-headed from lack of nourishment. Come on, maybe if I feed you, you'll regain your senses." Turning her around, he marched her down the hall.

As it was fairly late the dining room was almost deserted. Sitting across the table from him, Jen ate everything that was placed in front of her and tasted nothing, for Adam's eyes devoured her more thoroughly than his mouth devoured his food.

When they finished dinner they went into the bar to find Ted and Liz waiting for them at a table for four. On the table were four glasses, a full carafe of wine, and an almost empty one. Ted filled their glasses as they sat down.

"As you can see"—he indicated the empty carafe—"we've got a head start." Cocking one eyebrow he asked, "Where the hell did you two disappear to all day?" Adam's muttered "Mind your own business," combined with the bright flare of color that tinged Jen's cheeks, was all the answer he needed. With a murmured "Welcome to the club," to Jen, Ted lifted his glass in salute.

Their conversation was varied and far-ranging and flowed easily back and forth. In a surprisingly short amount of time she learned a lot about the others.

She learned that Ted was forty-three, a widower (which she already knew), had one child (a daughter), and was considering changing jobs as he was tired of being on the road all the time. He did woodworking as a hobby and admitted he was very good at it. He liked good food, quiet at-home nights, and Waylon Jennings's music.

Jen discovered that Liz, much to her surprise, was thirty-four, divorced, with no children. She worked in the reprographics department at Barton's and attended yoga exercise classes two nights a week. Liz admitted to being an opera buff who was happy as a clam to spend most of her evenings at home (a small apartment) listening to her large collection of opera recordings.

Although Jen already knew quite a bit about Adam, she found he liked cars (he owned two), skiing, all oceans, hiking, professional football—namely the Philadelphia Eagles—and history, from ancient to recent.

And the other three absorbed some things about Jen. Bits and pieces of information such as she was twenty-three, single, and lived at home with her parents. Also that she worked as a legal secretary, enjoyed most sports, loved live theater and old movies on TV, spent far too much money on clothes, and sang in the church choir.

A lull in the conversation came at the same time Ted poured the last of the wine. On his query of whether he should fight his way to the bar for a refill, Adam shook his head.

"Not for Jen and me, thanks." Standing up, he held his hand out to Jen. "We're going to fight our way onto the dance floor."

This time, when they reached the area set aside for dancing, Jen slid her arms around Adam's neck without hesitation.

"Good girl," he murmured against her hair as his arms circled her waist and drew her close to his body.

Enclosed in his embrace Jen lost all sense of time and surroundings. The music throbbing from the jukebox swirled through her mind and carried her to a distant, flat plateau which she and Adam were the sole occupants. Her face pressed to the side of his neck, eyes closed, she followed his lead around the minuscule floor, unaware of the couples around them.

"You look beautiful in that dress." Adam's warm, wine-scented breath ruffled the hair at her temple. His caressing tone ruffled every nerve in her body. "But I know you look even more beautiful out of it."

The ruffle swelled to a quivering wave that seemed to drain all the strength from her legs. Murmuring softly, Jen parted her lips and kissed his smooth, taut skin. His sharply indrawn breath was followed by the feel of his lips at the edge of her ear.

"Have you ever been in love, Jennifer?"

Adam's whispered question inserted a touch of reality into her dreamlike trance. Stirring restlessly, she sighed, "No." Then, with a deeper sigh, she lifted her head to look at him.

"I've had my share of crushes and infatuations," she confessed wryly. "But no, I've never been in love." Jen hesitated a moment, but she had to ask. "Have you?"

"I thought I was once," Adam replied, not hesitating at all. "It was a long time ago. While I was still in college. It was over before it ever really got started. That too turned out to be infatuation."

"I—" Suddenly nervous, Jen paused to swallow quickly. Was he trying to tell her that infatuation was all they had going between them now? Speaking carefully, she continued, "I suppose it is easy to confuse the two."

"I suppose so," Adam agreed quietly. "At least I've heard enough people say they weren't sure if they were in love."

Suddenly scared, Jen felt she couldn't breathe for a tightness compressing her chest. They had stopped even a pretense of dancing and were simply swaying to the music. Unable to take her eyes from his, Jen stared at Adam fearfully. When he finally spoke, it took several seconds for the meaning of his words to register in her mind.

"I'm sure." The hard finality in his tone caused Jen to go limp with relief. Her gaze steady on his, she said clearly, "So am I."

A bright flame flared in Adam's eyes, and his entire body went still for a moment before he released her with a whispered, "Come."

With meek acquiescence Jen preceded Adam off the dance floor, out of the bar, and across the lobby not knowing or caring how many pairs of eyes followed them knowingly.

With an outward composure that belied her mounting desire, she stood beside him calmly as he unlocked the door to his room. Adam himself appeared coolly unaffected as he pushed the door open and stood aside for her to enter.

The click of the lock automatically setting with the closing of the door was like an explosion that ripped away their facade of unconcern. Moving simultaneously, they reached for each other—tugging, yanking, pulling at each other's clothes.

Circling each other like hungry beasts, their movements jerky, their breathing ragged, they left a trail of crumpled, torn garments from the door to the bed where, divested of their cloaks of civilization, they grasped at each other savagely.

This time, their coming together held an element of violence. Imbued with a touch of madness in her need for him, Jen arched against his hard body wildly, teeth nipping, nails raking. As her body grew from warm to moist then slippery-wet from her frantic exertion, the soft moaning sounds in her throat grew into an outcry of sheer ecstasy that was echoed by Adam in the form of a harsh groan.

In sweet exhaustion, they lay side by side crosswise on

128

the bed as their labored breathing slowly returned to normal.

"Good God," Adam whispered shakily. "That was absolutely the wildest experience I've ever had."

Rising slightly, he leaned over her, his body supported by his forearm. Bending his head, he kissed her with a gentleness that bordered on reverence.

"You're perfect," he whispered as he leaned back to look at her. "An angel." A tender smile curved his lips. "My very own snow angel."

"Adam, I—" Jen could barely speak around the emotion clogging her throat. "I love you so much."

"You'd better," Adam growled, burying his face in her neck.

Jen felt his tongue glide over the fine gold chain that encircled her throat night and day. Lifting his head, Adam brought his hand up to finger the tiny loops.

"A gift from an admirer?" he asked tightly.

"No." Jen shook her head. "I bought it for myself over a year ago."

His fingers fumbled against her skin for several moments, and then he held the chain aloft.

"Loop it around my wrist," he ordered softly.

Without hesitation Jen took the chain from his fingers and did as he'd asked.

"Now you've chained me to you." Adam said with a smile when she'd fastened the clasp. "I'm yours to command. What's your pleasure, snow angel?"

The early-morning chill creeping over her naked flesh wakened Jen. The luminous hands on Adam's small travel alarm told her it was four thirty, and the air in the room was very cool.

A soft smile touched her lips at the half grunt, half snore that came from beside and slightly above her head. Turning her head, Jen studied the sleeping form that rested a few inches away from her. Adam lay sprawled on his back in an attitude of utter relaxation, one arm curved above his head, the other flung out to his side. His lips were slightly parted, and the taut skin that covered his face showed no sign of care or strain. On first sight, Jen had thought him handsome. Now, in his abandonment to oblivion, she thought him beautiful. Like countless number of lovers before her, Jen could find no fault in the object of her affection, for that beloved form had revealed to her a corner of heaven.

CHAPTER 8

"Somehow I've always known it would happen like this." Lisa's soft but liltingly happy voice dispelled Jen's bittersweet reverie. "Everyone has always laughed at my belief in love at first sight, but I knew that when I fell, it would be at once—and hard."

Shifting uncomfortably in the narrow seat, Jen tucked in her chin and hunched her shoulders in an unconsciously self-protective position. Biting on her lower lip, she squeezed her lids together in a vain attempt to contain the hot tears that slipped beneath her guard to roll down her cheeks.

The action of her searching fingers added force to the stinging flood. In times of tension or stress she had played with her chain not unlike people do with a rosary or worry beads. And now that source of comfort was denied her, for the chain was still around Adam's wrist. At least it had been when she'd slipped out of his bed, and his room, before daybreak, unable to face the thought of boldly walking through the lobby and encountering early-risers later in the morning.

Had Adam been aware of her going? Had he been feigning that posture of deep slumber? Although it hurt like hell, Jen now conceded the possibility that he had been. It had been around four forty-five when she'd returned to her own room. The desk clerk had said Adam had checked out just after six. One hour and twenty or twenty-five minutes at the outside, Jen sighed.

His phrasing in the note he'd left for her seemed to bear out her conjecturing. He'd written, Why did you go? Not, When did you go? Jen shivered. If he had been awake he had let her go believing he loved her. Love! Jen compressed her lips to keep from moaning aloud. She wanted —no, longed—to believe he *had* been asleep, *had* received an emergency call from home, really *had* no choice. She longed to believe that he *would* call her, *would* come to her as soon as he could, *would* prove to her that the blind trust she'd placed in him had not been betrayed.

She wanted to believe *all* these things, but the sense of betrayal, the feeling that she'd been used that had gripped her on first hearing he'd checked out of the motel, still nagged sickly at the back of her mind.

It was all too pat, had all came together too neatly, to be coincidence. Adam had to have realized, logically, that they would move on today, in one direction or another. God, she had made such a ridiculous ass of herself. Jen actually winced. After all her fast judgment making and moralizing, she had capitulated with an eagerness that was shaming, telling him, repeatedly, that she loved him.

Jen squirmed in her seat as the echo of her own strained voice, crying out the love words at a moment of sweetest agony, taunted her weary mind.

Was it possible Adam had chosen the path of least resistance? He was a man of the world. A man, Jen felt sure, who had known, and made love to, a number of women, all more beautiful and much more sophisticated than she could ever hope to be. And he had grown up with the belief that several lovers were acceptable—as long as one was selective. *And*—most searing thought of all—he had not actually said he was in love with her. With all the usual clarity of hindsight, Jen realized she had read what she'd wanted to believe into his avowed "I'm sure." Lord, for all she knew, he may have been thinking he was sure it was Friday.

Moving restlessly, Jen slid her hand into the slash pocket on the front of her jacket, her fingers curling around and crumpling the note Adam had left for her. At no time had he made any promises to her. *I will see you, I will call you,* hardly constituted a vow.

Wallowing in a quagmire of bitterness and despair, Jen stared sightlessly through the tinted glass window, totally oblivious to the murmur of conversation around her. Fingers mangling the envelope in her pocket, she thought distractedly, *Why didn't he, at least, toss my chain into the envelope?* She had had to save for months to buy it. She had seldom taken it off and felt naked without it. The absence of the gold circlet somehow intensified her feeling of rejection.

A tingling in the toes of a rapidly numbing foot alerted Jen to the necessity of shifting position once again. Drawn by discomfort out of her self-absorbtion, the rising note of excited chatter slowly registered in her mind.

Blinking away the remaining blur of moisture, Jen gazed out the window in surprise. The familiar environs of Norristown flashed by as the bus drew closer to Barton's—and home.

Cramped and both mentally and physically exhausted, Jen sighed with relief when Ted brought the large vehicle to a stop in almost the exact spot in the lot as he had early Thursday morning.

Had it only been two and a half days ago? Was it really possible that so much had happened in so short an amount of time? Jen heard her own silent questions voiced aloud from several sources.

"God, I can't believe I got on this bus, right here, just two days ago." This from a man near the front of the bus who was standing in the aisle and unconcernedly massaging his rump.

"I feel like I've been away for weeks." This was from the whining woman across from Jen. "And confined to this damned seat for most of that time."

"If I don't get something to eat soon, I'm going to

133

expire right here in this bus." This from the ever hungry Terry.

"May I have your attention, please?" Liz's voice, magnified by the PA system, silenced the chatter. "I am sorry to have to inform you that there is every possibility you will all be receiving a bill for your lodging at the motel."

This statement was met by a barrage of angry exclamations.

"What?"

"Why?"

"The trip was paid for, dammit!"

"What the hell are you trying to pull?"

The last remark was followed immediately by Liz's exasperatedly snapped "If you will be quiet, I'll explain."

The melee subsided to a few disgruntled grumbles.

"Believe me, I understand how you feel," Liz assured them. "And as the gentleman pointed out, the trip *was* paid for." Liz paused to add emphasis to her next words. "It was paid *in full* to the ski lodge. During a three-way phone conversation this morning between our travel agency, Bill Wakefield, and me, arrangements were made to pay the motel bill." Liz paused to draw a quick breath before continuing. "We will, of course, be contacting the management at the ski lodge. If they will agree to a partial refund, it may be enough to cover the motel bill. But please understand that they are not required by law to make any refund."

"But it wasn't our fault we couldn't make it to the lodge!" Not surprisingly, the shrill protest came from the woman across the aisle from Jen.

"Nor was it theirs," Liz shot back angrily. Then more calmly, she added, "I'm sorry. I understand how you all must feel, but there is nothing I can do about it. Now, Ted has asked me to tell you that driving is still very hazardous, so please be careful on your way home."

Jen sat with outward patience while the muttering group filed out of the bus. At that moment the thought of possibly receiving a bill—or the death sentence—left her emotionally untouched. All she wanted was to get off the bus, get into her car, and get home as quickly as she safely could.

Saying good-bye to Liz and Ted turned out to be less difficult than Jen had feared it would be. As she stepped out of the bus she was caught and pulled against Ted in a bear hug.

"Take care of yourself, honey," Ted growled into her ear softly. "Keep the faith, Jen. *I* believe Adam will get in touch with you. You must try and believe it too."

Jen blinked against the renewed sting in her eyes. "I want to believe it, Ted," she choked as she disentangled herself from his arms. "I really do, but—"

"Don't even think *but,*" Liz urged. "Think positive." She gave Jen a quick hug, then said briskly, "Now, go home and get some rest—you look beat. And call me soon—okay?"

"Yes, I will. I promise." Jen somehow managed a natural smile. "Drive carefully, both of you."

With a last wave of her hand, Jen picked up her suitcase and walked to her still snow-laden car. Thankfully Barton's maintenance crew had cleared the lot around the car, so all Jen had to do was clean the windows, back and front. Thirty nerve-racking minutes after she drove off the Barton's lot, Jen pulled onto the narrow driveway to the one-car garage attached to her parents' rambling ranch home. It was at that moment she remembered she'd promised her mother she'd call the day before.

Her mother, obviously, had not forgotten. She met Jen at the front door, a frown of disapproval marring her usually serene face.

"Jennifer Louise Lengle." Ella's use of Jen's full name was a clear indication of how upset she was. "Do you have any idea how worried your father and I have been? Why didn't you call?"

Even as she scolded, Ella's eyes grew sharp with concern as they noted Jen's pale cheeks and the dark shadows under her eyes.

"I'm sorry, Mom." Standing just inside the door on the mat her ever tidy mother had placed there for the purpose of removing sloppy wet clothes and boots, Jen bent listlessly to tug at the zipper of her boot. "I have no excuse. I simply forgot."

Although Jen didn't notice, the look of concern spread from her mother's eyes to her entire face. "Jennifer"— Ella's tone of annoyance was gone, replaced by anxiety— "are you feeling all right?"

Her boots dealt with, Jen straightened. "I'm just tired." She smiled reassuringly as she shrugged out of her jacket. "And I think I may be coming down with a cold." This last remark she tacked on in an effort to stave off questions about her puffy, red-rimmed eyes. "Where's Daddy?"

A soft smile curved her mother's lips as she plucked the jacket out of Jen's hands and turned to hang it in the closet. "In his 'den,' asleep in front of the TV." Turning back to Jen, she ordered gently, "Leave your suitcase where it is for now and come have a cup of tea. You look like you need it."

As she followed her mother to the kitchen, Jen glanced down the long hall that lead to the home's four bedrooms, a reflection of her mother's soft smile on her own lips. Her father's "den," as her mother had laughingly dubbed it, was located in the smallest of the bedrooms. Before her sister Vicki's marriage, the room had been used as a guest room. But two weeks after the wedding Ella began rearranging the rooms. Declaring, teasingly, that she was tired of listening to her husband snore as he ostensibly watched television, she turned Vicki's room into a guest room and installed a desk, portable television, and a lounge chair into the small room and christened it "Dad's den."

The aroma of Yankee pot roast assailed Jen's nostrils as she entered the large kitchen, and with a surprised glance at the wall clock, Jen saw it was only a half hour shy of the usual dinner hour of six o'clock. *Lord!* Jen grimaced as she dropped onto a plastic and chrome kitchen chair. No wonder she felt wrung out. They had been on that bus all day!

"Did you run into any difficulty on the way home?" Ella asked as she placed a steaming cup of tea in front of Jen.

"No," Jen shook her head. "But it was slow going. We left the motel around ten this morning."

"There's my girl." Ralph Lengle's warm voice preceded him into the kitchen. Coming to a stop beside her chair, he slid an arm around her shoulders and gave her a brief hug. "Your trip turned out to be pretty much of a fiasco, didn't it?" he commiserated softly.

In more ways than one, Jen thought tiredly. Glancing up at him, she smiled ruefully. "I'm afraid so."

Becoming still, his eyes searched hers knowingly. For as long as she could remember, her father had been able to gauge her state of health—emotional and physical—from her eyes. Now he seemed puzzled. "What's up, Jen?" he probed gently. "Aren't you feeling well? Or is something troubling you?"

"I'm okay, Daddy." Jen shook her head, as much to deny the moisture gathering in her eyes as his words. Always susceptible to his caring gentleness, Jen was even more so now. "I think I may have caught a cold."

Even though her father nodded, his expression left little doubt in Jen's mind that he was unconvinced.

Somehow Jen managed to eat at least some of her dinner and get through the clearing-away period after the meal was finished. When she was finally free to go to her own room, she walked down the hall determined to take a hot bath, crawl into bed, and have a good cry in an attempt to dissolve the tight knot of misery that had settled in her chest. She achieved the first two of her objectives, but after slipping between the covers, she was dead to the world before the first tear could fully form.

Uncomfortably for Jen, her hasty assurances to her

parents that she was coming down with a cold proved to be prophetic. By Monday morning she was sneezing at the rate of what seemed to be three times within every five minutes; bleary-eyed; and red-nosed from her tender skin's constant contact with a procession of tissues. All that long week, Jen dragged her aching body from home to office to home again, sneezing and sniffling all the way.

Dousing herself with hot baths, aspirin, and a supposed-ly bracing tea concoction her mother brewed for her every night, Jen steadfastly refused to see a doctor. By the end of the week the sneezing and sniffling had stopped, but Jen felt exhausted and looked, in her mother's words, like warmed-over death. Even though her mother had made the statement teasingly, her eyes had revealed her growing concern. Jen had to fight the urge to confide in her mother, then have a good cry on her shoulder.

But she didn't. As each successive day passed without word from Adam, the fear grew inside Jen that she would never hear from him again. How could she tell her mother about him? What could she say? There was no way she could explain what had happened in that snowed-in motel. How could she make her mother understand when she didn't quite understand it herself?

Jen spent the entire week silently fighting the doubts that assailed her mind. Had she fallen headlong into love, she wondered over and over again, or had she been caught up into the snow fever Ted had talked about? Away from Adam's hypnotic, warm velvet gaze, his bone-melting touch, and his reason-destroying mouth, Jen was left with the knowledge of her own inexperience.

Had she, in her innocence, allowed herself to be led down the garden path? Had she, to be blunt, allowed herself to be used as a convenience—a bed and body warmer? The self-questioning seared her soul, but though she struggled to banish them, the questions persisted.

Never before in her life had she encountered anyone like Adam Banner. He was a completely unknown quantity to her, different from any other man Jen had ever came in contact with. His upbringing and his life-style were the complete antitheses of her own.

Jen was, she knew, very much a product of the everyday middle class. Her own upbringing had been free of any disruptive influences or emotional upheavals. As she had honestly told Adam, she was very like other people.

Her moral code had been instilled by loving, concerned, God-fearing parents who believed in the sanctity of the marriage vows. The idea of divorce was unpalatable to them, but compared to divorce, infidelity was blasphemy. Jen had absorbed and accepted their beliefs unquestioningly. It was therefore unsurprising that she had been shocked at Adam's revelations. And now her own response to him held equal shock value.

As one day dragged itself into another, her head cold drained her energy, and her confusing thoughts ravaged her mind, Jen felt torn in two by conflicting conclusions.

On the one hand was the emotional realization that what had been ignited inside her at the first touch of Adam's eyes had not been infatuation or mere physical attraction but the first, exciting spark of love—a spark that had flared into a vociferous flame, consuming all other considerations, by the time Adam's note had been handed to her.

On the other hand was the daunting voice of reason that told her that even if he were with her, they would be poles apart. Even though she was young, her character mold was set. Her dreams had been of a very prosaic nature. Very simply, she wanted a life like her mother had: a companionable relationship with her husband, a comfortable home, and children to love and enjoy.

By Friday morning Jen had reached the heartbreaking conclusion that even if Adam should still call or come to her, they had no future together. She loved him—almost desperately so—and she ached to be in his arms, to have all rational thought burned out of her mind by his searching mouth. But she knew that when his arms loosened and his lips left hers, the cold light of reality would still be there, glaringly exposing the fact that although opposites often attract, they are as often incompatible.

Sadly, Jen came to the decision that should he contact her, she would have to deny her feelings for him, for she truly believed that if she didn't, she would pay for a long time to come.

When Chris called while Jen was on her lunch break, she was so weary of her own thoughts she answered "Yes" at once, when Chris asked if she wanted to go out that evening.

"It'll be the usual crowd," Chris said lightly. "At the usual place."

The usual place was a local night spot, frequented mostly by young singles.

"I'll be there," Jen promised firmly, suddenly filled with a need to get back into the normal swing of her life.

Jen informed her parents of her plans over the dinner table, feeling a twinge of guilt at the relief that washed over her mother's face. She had been aware of her mother's concern, of course, but now the full extent of that concern was clearly visible.

She should have known, Jen chided herself. She and Vicki had never been able to hide anything from their mother, and although her mother had no way of knowing what was troubling her, it was obvious she was aware Jen was suffering from more than a common cold.

"It'll do you a world of good," Ella declared with a forced note of cheer in her voice.

"Other than to go back and forth to work, you've been cooped up in the house all week."

After dinner, having cleared the table and stacked the dishwasher, Jen and her mother were straightening the dining area when the phone rang.

"I'll get it," her father offered, coming in the back door after taking out the trash, and crossing the kitchen to the wall phone. Jen was bent over the table replacing the flower-ringed candle centerpiece when he called, "It's for you, honey."

Knowing Chris's genius for changing plans at the last minute, Jen was wondering what the change might be as she took the receiver from her father and said, "Hello?"

"Jennifer?"

CHAPTER 9

The low, caressing sound of her name froze Jen in place. She was unaware that her parents had left the dining room. She did not hear the sound of the TV being turned up in the living room. For long seconds she could not think or hear or breathe.

"Jennifer?" Not so low now, Adam's sharp tone shattered her trancelike state.

Placing her hand over the end of the receiver, Jen drew a deep, ragged breath and released it slowly before removing her hand and answering huskily, "Yes?"

"Darling, you sound strange. Are you all right?" Adam asked in the same sharp tone.

"Yes, I'm fine. I've had a cold all week, but it's better now," Jen explained away the husky sound of her voice.

"Dammit," Adam muttered. "I kept you out in the snow too long last week. Have you seen a doctor?"

"No, it wasn't necessary." Jen sighed. "It was only a head cold, Adam," she ended somewhat abruptly. Why were they talking about a head cold! Adam was quiet a moment and when his voice again touched her ear it held that low, caressing note that so affected her nervous system.

"I'm hungry for you, darling," he murmured roughly. "Cold or no cold, contagious or not, I want to kiss you so badly I get the shakes just thinking about it."

His blatantly sensual tone scattered the fog blanketing

her mind, and with a start Jen remembered her decision of that morning.

"Did Bill give you my note, angel?" Adam's soft tone broke into her thoughts.

"Yes," Jen answered flatly.

"Jennifer, are you angry about the suddenness of my departure?" All traces of the sensuality were gone now, replaced by tight urgency. "There was a good reason for the abruptness of my actions."

"I'm sure there was," Jen replied in the same flat tone. And she really was sure, but somehow it didn't seem important anymore. If she was going to stick to her decision, the less she knew, the better. Forcing all expression from her voice, she murmured, "It's not important, Adam."

"Not important?" he repeated blankly. Then he almost shouted, "What do you mean, not important? And why isn't it?"

"Why is it?" she asked quietly.

"Why?" he repeated incredulously. "Wait a minute," he went on with forced control, "I'm tired, and I've got jet lag, and I think I'm missing something." He drew a long breath, then went on slowly, "Why isn't it important, Jennifer?"

"Because"—Jen swallowed around the painful tightness in her throat—"because what happened between us at that motel shouldn't have."

"Oh, hell," Adam groaned. "She's been passing judgments again—this time on herself," he muttered before demanding, "Is that why you left my room that morning?"

"That's not important either anymore," Jen sighed.

"Jennifer, listen to me," Adam said impatiently. "You're being ridiculous and childish. We have to talk about this."

His calling her ridiculous and childish stirred defensive anger in Jen. What did he want of her? Why was he even bothering? First he'd accused her of being too quick to judge. Then he'd scolded her for being tactless. Soon after that he'd called her narrow-minded and straitlaced. Now she was ridiculous and childish. The list of her character faults seemed to grow longer and longer. Why was he even interested? In comparison to the other women he knew, especially his mother, she had to appear appallingly gauche. That thought seared her mind and loosened her tongue in retaliation.

"I don't understand you at all, Adam," Jen cried through stiff lips. "Why did you call me? What interest can you have in such a morally uptight juvenile?"

"Dammit, Jennifer"—Adam's rough tone betrayed his anger—"will you stop this stupidity—"

"No, damn you, Adam." Jen's knuckles were white from gripping the receiver. Now she was stupid! The list grew longer every time he opened his mouth. God, what a bore he must find her. But then—why? The answer came glaringly simple. She had been so unbelievably easy. Was it possible he was between women, she thought wildly, and needed a diversion? The thought was crushing, and without actually forming them, words of repudiation poured from her trembling lips.

"I may be stupid and childish, but I'm not a complete idiot, even if I have given you reason to believe I am. I am not interested in being a part-time playmate to be used whenever there's a lull in your more sophisticated action."

A long silence followed her nearly incoherent tirade, during which Jen could only boggle at her own outrageous statement. She was wrong; she *was* a complete idiot! The bark of Adam's harsh laughter seemed to indicate his concurrence.

"Part-time playmate!" His laughter turned derisive. "You've been reading too many women's magazines, young lady. I'm coming up there so we can hash this out."

"I won't be here."

"Where are you going?" Adam demanded. "Who are you going with?"

Jen bristled at his sharply possessive tone. How dare he question her?

Enraged, Jen choked, "None of your damned business," and slammed the receiver onto its cradle.

Shaken, trembling, Jen stood staring at the phone, fully expecting it to ring again. As the seconds dragged into minutes her shoulders drooped, and she had to close her eyes against the hot sting of tears. Leaning tiredly against the wall, Jen berated herself for the moisture that trickled from under her tightly closed lids.

A shudder rippled through her body as an echo of his voice whispered through her mind: "Jennifer, are you angry?" Angry? Good Lord, if it was only that simple. How much easier it would be if the only emotion she felt was healthy anger. She ached to see him, ached to be in his arms, while at the same time she was afraid to see him. She wasn't sure she could trust him not to hurt her again.

Sighing for what might have been, she pushed herself away from the wall. She had taken three steps across the inlaid tile floor when a sudden thought brought her up short. Once before she had thought her words had driven him away. His reply to her then had been "I'll never walk away from you," and Jen knew now, positively, that before long he would be there, at her home, insisting she listen to him.

The thought generated action, and Jen practically ran down the hall to her room. She had over an hour until she was to meet Chris and the rest of her friends, but as she had no idea where Adam had been calling from, she could not, now, waste any time hanging around the house. She had to get ready as quickly as possible and get out. For if she saw him, if he got his hands on her, her resistance would dissolve in her need of him.

Eleven minutes later, every nerve in her body quivering, Jen backed her car out of the driveway. Instead of the long, hot bath she had looked forward to, she had made do with a quick sponge bath and a fresh application of makeup. A shimmery, clingy jumpsuit had replaced her tailored office clothes, and her comfortable low-heeled pumps had been exchanged for a few straps attached to a thin sole and narrow spike heels. She had shrugged into her short fake fur jacket as she headed for the door and had forestalled the questions she could see forming on her mother's lips with a brightly chirped, "I gotta run. Don't worry. I will not drink too much, I will drive carefully, and I won't be very late. Bye." Her last word coincided with the closing of the door.

Jen's breathing didn't return to normal until she was several blocks away from her home. Still shaky, she jerked to a stop as a light changed to red, and she sat gripping the steering wheel, wondering what in the world she was going to do for an hour. A short blast of the horn from the car behind her made her aware that the light had switched to green. It also made her aware of her distracted state of mind. *Better go to Chris's,* she told herself scathingly. *In the condition I'm in, I'm a menace on the road.*

Chris met her at the door with a frown and a wailed "Did I screw things up again?"

"What do you mean?" Jen asked blankly, her thoughts still on her rush to escape.

"Roger is picking me up." Chris bit her lip. "I thought you said you'd meet us at the club."

At that moment Jen blessed Chris's absentmindedness and her penchant for "screwing things up."

"That's okay." She managed to produce a careless laugh. "I'll follow you and Roger, no major problem."

By the time they arrived at the night spot hangout, Jen had herself under control—at least on the surface. The others were already there and had pushed several tables together to accommodate the group that totaled ten.

Friday night—and the atmosphere was pure party, not only at their table but throughout the large room. The

146

throbbing beat of the loud music, combined with the equally loud conversation and laughter, made thinking an impossibility for which Jen was grateful.

Laughing, joking, drinking, Jen threw herself into the spirit of revelry with a frenzy of desperation—although her drinking was limited. She had gulped down a glass and a half of gin and tonic when Roger literally dragged her onto the dance floor.

The colored, diffused lighting that bounced over and around the dance floor blended perfectly with the blare of rock music. What Roger lacked in expertise he more than made up for in enthusiasm. When, at the end of the forth energetic number, Jen laughingly cried "Uncle," her already clingy jumpsuit was plastered to her perspiration-wet body in spots, and her face glowed with a moist sheen.

Still laughing as they walked off the dance floor, Jen lifted her head to glance around the room and felt her body go stiff with shock. Adam was standing with his back to the bar, his eyes fastened on her. The moment she saw him, he pushed himself lazily away from the bar and started slowly toward her.

Her first thought was to run, followed immediately by, where to? Adam's expression, hard with grim determination, brought her faltering steps to a halt. Forcing a semblance of lightness to her tone, she said, "Go ahead, Roger, I see someone I know," just as the lights dimmed and the strains of a ballad filled the room. All her senses centered on the man approaching her, Jen didn't even hear Roger's reply or see him move away.

When he reached her he slid his arms around her waist and without saying a word drew her into the midst of the slowly moving couples. Without a thought, Jen's arms moved to circle his neck, and she felt a hot shaft of excitement as his arms tightened.

"Jennifer."

The familiar, longed for, whispered caress robbed her of all rational thought. Without even a pretense of dancing,

147

Adam held her tightly against his hard body, swaying gently in time with the music. He didn't speak, but then he didn't have to; his body spoke volumes. And her body answered: yes, yes, yes.

One slow song followed another, all unheard by Jen. The darting colored lights that signaled the return to up-beat music pierced the mist of sensuousness clouding Jen's reason. Pulling away from him in disgust, she made a zigzag dash off the dance floor, half afraid he'd follow her, half afraid he wouldn't. He didn't, and Jen was back at the table several minutes before she found the courage to look around for him.

He was gone! Her eyes wide with disbelief, Jen made a second, slower search of the room even though she knew she would not have missed him on the first circuit. He simply was not there. Like a phantom conjured up by her imagination, he had disappeared. Fighting an eerie feeling of unreality, she gripped her glass with trembling fingers, unaware and unconcerned with the bantering chatter of her friends.

Other than to whisper her name, he had not spoken, had made no attempt to get her alone. Her face grew warm with anger and humiliation at the memory of how effort-lessly he'd drawn a physical response from her. But why the disappearing act?

"Jen, are you feeling all right?"

Chris's sharp tone penetrated Jen's self-absorbtion before she could formulate an answer to her own silent question.

"Yes, of course." Jen smiled shakily. "But I'm suddenly very tired." It was true; she suddenly did feel very, very tired. "I think I'll go home to bed—it's been a long day."

The instant response of every male in the group to go with her was almost Jen's undoing. Swallowing painfully against the constricting tightness in her throat, she shook her head in rejection of their offers while choking out a none-too-articulate "Thank you."

148

Emerging from the building, Jen shuddered and hunched her shoulders against the sting of the cold night air on her overheated body. Clutching her upturned collar under her chin, she hurried to the protection of her car.

Her mind scurried from one inane, unrelated thought to another all the way home in a desperate but vain attempt to avoid thinking of Adam. Under all the surface thoughts unanswerable questions hammered away relentlessly. How had he known where she'd be? Why had he disappeared as soon as they'd left the dance floor? Why had he remained silent when only a few hours earlier he'd insisted she listen to him? Where had he gone? And—damn him— what kind of game was he playing anyway?

By the time she turned onto the driveway and parked in front of the garage, she was too tired to notice the car parked along the curb in front of her home. As she stepped onto the macadam, the motion of the passenger door swinging open caught her attention. At the same instant she recognized the gold Formula, she heard Adam's softly voiced order. "Come get in the car, Jennifer."

For one brief moment Jen considered ignoring him and making a dash for the front door. In the very next moment she dismissed the idea, certain he'd simply lie on the doorbell until she admitted him. The lone light left on in the living room gave evidence that her parents were in bed, and Jen did not want them disturbed. She didn't want to answer a lot of questions about Adam either.

Moving with obvious reluctance, she covered the ground to his car. "What do you want?" she whispered harshly.

"Get in the car," Adam repeated patiently.

"No."

"Why not?" he asked, still very patiently.

"I don't want to hear whatever it is you have to say." Jen heard his sharply indrawn breath and went on, "I don't trust you, Adam."

Adam was quiet for long seconds, then, in a very even,

very quiet tone promised, "If you don't get in the car—now—I will get out and put you in."

Deciding to be prudent, Jen slid onto the seat next to him, letting her anger show by slamming the door shut. Eyes blazing, voice frigid, she faced him squarely.

"All right, Adam, say your little piece—if you must."

"I don't think so."

"What?" Jen frowned at his flat, uncompromising tone.

"You may get out of the car, Jennifer." His tone was still flat, but carried an inflection that tugged at Jen's memory. What was it? Unable to grasp the elusive memory, Jen shook her head.

"But—then why—"

"Why waste my time—and yours?"

The inflection was stronger now, and suddenly Jen was back in the motel, hearing him say "Are you still mad at me?" in the same somewhat sad tone. At that time she had hurt Liz with her hasty condemnation. Was Adam hurt? Was it possible she had misjudged his actions? Had she, again, been too hasty? Hasty? After all *his* words of condemnation of her? Again Jen shook her head.

"Are you going to get out?" Adam's quiet voice ended her introspection. Glancing at him, Jen was struck by an odd, waiting stillness about him. *Waiting for what?* Jen wondered confusedly.

"Adam, I— What are you doing?"

What he was doing was sliding his hand around her neck as he leaned across the console dividing the seats. Bending his head, he muttered, "You should have got out while you had the chance." His lips brushed the skin in front of her ear. Although the touch was feather-light, Jen could not repress the shiver that rippled through her, or the half gasp, half moan that whispered through her lips.

"Or didn't you *really* want to get out?" Adam's breath tickled her face as his lips moved from her ear to the corner of her mouth.

"Yes—no—I—ooh!"

Adam's mouth slid over her parted lips, silencing her vain attempt to answer him. It didn't matter. Nothing mattered except the wildfire that spread through her veins and sent her mind whirling. He was here. He was now. And everything else was, for the moment, forgotten in her body's clamoring response.

"Jennifer, Jennifer."

First against her lips, then against her cheek—over and over again—her name was whispered huskily as his lips explored her face. The overpowering need to touch him drove her hands to his head, sent her fingers spearing through the toast-brown strands. His hand at the back of her head urged her closer, closer.

"God, I've missed you." His tongue skipped along the edge of her ear. "Missed this," he groaned, trailing that tip of fire to her lips. "I want to touch you, kiss you, all over. Wet my lips for me, darling." The urgent whisper was followed by his hand cupping her breast.

An alarm went off in Jen's head, restoring reason and cooling her overheated senses. Turning her face away from the temptation of his mouth, his words, Jen cried, "Adam, don't!"

Long fingers gripped convulsively, painfully, at her breast an instant before the hand was lifted to grasp her chin. Lifting his head, he tersely ordered, "Look at me, Jennifer." Without waiting for her to comply he forced her to face him.

"What do you mean—'Adam, don't'?" he asked harshly. "Adam, don't at all, or not here?"

"Not—not at all." Why did her voice lack conviction? Why now? Jen groaned silently. Now, when she had to make it clear to him that she would not allow him to use her again. Letting her hands drop into her lap, she clasped them together, drew a quick, strengthening breath and added, "I told you earlier that I'm not interested in being a part-time playmate. And even if you think it's funny, I mean it."

"Oh, you're wrong, I don't think it's funny at all." Leaning back, he pinned her with a challenging stare. "How about being a full-time playmate?"

"What—exactly—do you mean?" Jen asked warily.

"I can't keep my hands off you and you know it." That strangely sad smile touched his lips fleetingly. "And, although you'll probably deny it, you can't keep your hands off me, either. There's only one thing for us—isn't there?"

Jen was almost afraid to ask, yet of course she had to.

"And that is?"

"Marriage."

Open-mouthed, wide-eyed, Jen sat staring at him, too stunned to speak. When, finally, she did find her voice, all she could manage was a croaked "Marriage?"

"Do you have a better solution?" he asked imperturbably.

"But we don't even know each other. We—" She was going to add that they had nothing in common, but Adam's roar of laughter drowned her surprised protest.

"Don't know each other?" Still laughing, he shook his head in disbelief. "Jennifer, we know every inch of each other."

"I don't mean *that* way." Stung, Jen flung the words at him.

"In case you don't know, *that* way is the most important way," he retorted. Grasping her shoulders, he gave her a gentle shake. "We have all the time in the world to explore each other's personalities, innocent one. And, personally, I'd prefer to do it in bed." Pulling her to him, he kissed her hungrily. "I think we'd better get married, angel. Very soon."

"H—How soon?" Jen whispered around the tightness in her throat.

"Next week?"

"Next week? Adam, are you out of your mind?" Jen gasped.

"Not yet," he murmured against her lips. "But I'm getting pretty close to it with wanting you." Drawing her as close to his body as the console would allow, his lips teased hers while his hands moved restlessly over her shoulders and down her back. "Why not next week?" he asked in a near growl.

Why? Where could she start? She didn't even know where he'd be after next week—or before, for that matter. Did he? she wondered fleetingly. To her, the way he lived seemed unstable and erratic. In no way could she see herself fitting into his life. What did they have, really, except this crazy physical attraction?

"Jennifer?" The whispered caress, combined with the mind-clouding, restless movements of his hands on her body destroyed her attempt at marshaling arguments. His lips almost touching hers crumbled her defenses entirely. "I said, why not next week?"

Jen blurted the first thing that came into her mind. "My parents! Adam, they haven't even met you." Pulling away from him, she wailed, "What on earth could I say to them?"

"How about the truth?" Adam murmured, moving back onto his own seat behind the wheel.

"What truth?" Jen asked uneasily.

"Why, while snowbound, you met a man, fell in love, and went to bed with him." Jen gasped, but Adam went on in a soft, rough tone, "Or have you forgotten you said you were in love?"

"No," she denied swiftly. "I haven't forgotten."

"Neither have I. Are you going to marry me, Jennifer?"

Every one of the reasons why she should say no rushed into her mind, only to become muddled and confused, and rendered useless against one irrefutable fact. She wanted him so very badly. Could it possibly work? If, given a little time to get to know each other—would it? Maybe, hope sprang wildly, just maybe. She tried to visualize the future, but the only· image that came was of the two of them, locked together, on the bed in his room at the motel.

The picture made her heart thump, filled every inch of her being with need. *No!* she thought frantically. *That's not enough to build a future on. But—but if I can keep him at arm's length, at a distance, while we get to know each other? Could it work? I've got to give it a try, because I love him. Oh, God, how I love him.*

"Well?"

Jen started at the impatient edge in Adam's voice. She had been quiet too long, and he wanted an answer—at once.

"Yes," Jen surrendered.

"When?" Adam demanded.

"Adam, you must understand, planning a wedding takes time."

"How much time?" Adam asked grimly.

Jen wet her lips. "My mother would love a June wedding."

"Four months." His lips twisted wryly. "And you fully intend making me sweat out every day of it, don't you?" Before she could answer he sighed, "Is this to be some kind of a test?" But again he didn't wait for a reply. "Okay, four months. I have some things to clear up anyway."

"What things?" she asked in confusion.

"Jennifer"—his voice held rough impatience—"do you want a husband that spends most of the year out of the country?"

"No, of course not!"

"That's what I thought. I'm changing jobs." Jen opened her mouth to question him, and he held up his hand to forestall her. "Not companies, Jennifer, just the job I do for that company. I've been offered a desk job several times over the last few years, and now I've decided to take it. But I will have to leave the country a few times before June."

Who is she? Jen hated herself for the first question that flashed into her mind. Nevertheless, there it was, and she had to face it; he was a very virile man. He had proved that—repeatedly—in a very short amount of time. The mental question that followed was equally as unsettling. Would he break with her entirely or—afraid even to think of an answer, she rushed into speech with the first thing that came into her head.

"Where are we going to live?"

"That's one of the other things I was thinking of." Adam glanced at her sharply, frowning, then he went on calmly, "I have a town house outside Philly." He named a rather exclusive suburb, causing Jen to raise her eyebrows in surprise. "If it doesn't suit you, we'll look around for something else." He shrugged. "But we can discuss all that later. Right now it's late and you'd better go in. I have to go into the office tomorrow morning to work on a report, but I'll call you after lunch, okay?"

Feeling suddenly very tired, Jen nodded and turned to the door, her hand groping for the release.

"No good-night kiss, Jennifer?" Adam chided softly.

Jen turned to meet his descending head with an eagerness that was shaming, her arms curling around his neck at the same moment his hands slid under her short jacket to clasp her waist. His mouth explored hers with an almost cool deliberation. She sensed it and still she was powerless against the fierce surge of desire that drove her lips to beg him silently to deepen the kiss. When his hands moved up her sides to brush the outer curve of her breasts, Jen shivered in anticipation. Sharp disappointment drew a soft moaning protest from her lips when his hands moved back to her waist.

"My foolish angel." Adam's warm breath feathered her cheek deliciously as his lips sought her ear. "In punishing me, you'll be punishing yourself—don't you see that?"

"I don't know what you mean," Jen denied softly.

"I cautioned you once about lying to yourself." As if to underline his words, his hands slid over the silklike material of her jumpsuit, tantalizingly near but not touching her breasts until she, in an aching need to feel the possession of those hands, arched her back. "You need it"—one long finger drew a curving line up to a quivering tip—"every bit as badly as I do. If you persist with your present attitude, these next four months are going to be sheer hell—for both of us."

Anger at him as well as herself gave her the strength to tear herself out of his arms. What he'd said was true, of course, which made it that much harder to swallow. How, she wondered distractedly, had he known so positively that she had no intention of allowing that kind of intimacy again before the marriage took place? Feeling guilty—and made more angry for feeling so—she snapped, "You're wrong, Adam. I will be much too busy to think about it."

"Oh, you'll think about it." Adam's soft laughter fanned the flame of her anger. "In fact, I'll bet that by the time *the* day dawns, you will be thinking of little else."

"No!" Jen shook her head sharply. "I—"

"But console yourself with this thought," Adam interrupted harshly. "By then, I will have been on the rack for a very long time."

Refusing to listen to any more, Jen found the release and let the door swing open. "I can't think how I'll explain to my parents." The sudden thought flashed into her head and emerged as a wail.

"I'm not going to disappear into a puff of smoke, Jennifer," Adam laughed softly. "I don't expect you to face them with this alone. Don't say anything until I can get here tomorrow."

"Adam!" Jen twisted around to him fearfully. "You won't tell them what happened between us? They have—certain ideas—rigid ones—and—and—" Jen floundered, her mouth going dry at the thought of her parents' reaction to that kind of news.

"I'm not a complete bastard, Jennifer," Adam ground out fiercely. "I don't make love—and tell."

Jen stared at him wide-eyed. Oh, Lord, how could they hope to make a life together when they became bogged down with misunderstanding at the first hurdle? She had been afraid that, in his honesty, he would be a little too frank with her parents. While he thought—what? That she believed him capable of viciousness? The very idea shocked her into stuttered speech.

"Adam, I—I didn't mean—"

The hard, unrelenting set of his features told her her plea wasn't reaching him.

"I know exactly what you meant." Then, his tone crushing, he turned and grasped the wheel. "Good night, Jennifer."

Feeling casually dismissed, her cheeks hot with embarrassment, Jen got out of the car, closing the door carefully.

Forcing herself to maintain a normal pace, she walked to the front door, unlocked it with trembling fingers, and slipping inside, stood shaking like a leaf as she listened to the sound of Adam's car fade as he drove away.

Over an hour later, unable to sleep, Jen finally gave up her fitful tossing—and the effort not to think. After fighting her way out of the tangle of covers, she pushed her feet into furry mules and went slapping along the hallway to the kitchen.

She was pouring herself a glass of milk she didn't really want when her mother entered the kitchen. Wondering vaguely if a feather could fall to the floor without her mother hearing it, Jen sat down at the table and stared broodingly into the white liquid.

"What's the matter, honey?" Ella asked quietly. "Couldn't you sleep?"

"No." Jen shook her head briefly before glancing up. "I'm sorry if I disturbed you."

"Oh, Jen," Ella sighed, "you've disturbed me all week. Your lack of appetite, your listlessness, your sleeplessness. Oh, yes"—she looked squarely into Jen's widened eyes—"I've known all week that you haven't been sleeping well." Her voice went low, coaxing. "Can't you tell me what's bothering you?"

Jen stared into her mother's concerned face for a long time, then, shifting her gaze back to her glass, she whispered, "There's this man."

"Ahhh—" Ella expelled her breath slowly. "I was somehow sure that there was. You met him while you were away?"

"Yes."

"He was a passenger on the bus?"

"No."

"Jen, will you look at me?" her mother ordered impatiently. "I do not like being cast in the role of interrogator. Now, if you want to talk about it, then talk. If not, say so, and I'll go back to bed."

Immediately contrite, Jen grasped her mother's hand. "I'm sorry, Mom," she apologized. Then, coming to a swift decision, blurted, "He's asked me to marry him."

"And are you going to?"

Stunned by her mother's calmly voiced question, Jen gaped at her in astonishment.

"Well?" Ella prompted softly. "Are you?"

"Yes, but—" Jen's expression betrayed her bewilderment. "Is that all you have to say?"

"Hardly," Ella laughed. "But I wanted a definite answer before I bombarded you with questions."

They talked for nearly an hour over steaming cups of tea her mother insisted on making after pouring the untouched milk down the drain. Thankfully her mother's questions did not probe too deeply, and with a sigh of relief, Jen willingly answered all of them.

By the time they bade each other a whispered "Good night," her mother knew what Adam looked like, what he did for a living, where he lived, and that Jen loved him very much. What she did not know was how impetuously Jen had responded to him, or any of the intimate, hurtful details that followed.

It was not until Jen was back in bed and beginning to drift into sleep that two thoughts—springing into her mind back to back—made her shift position restlessly. The first thought was what she would do if, after the way they'd parted, Adam did not call her. The second was much more irrelevant. Did he still have her chain? Not having the answer to either question, and by now dead tired, Jen closed her eyes tightly and fell asleep.

Jen's first thought on waking at ten thirty was an echo of the one held while falling asleep. Would he call? The very real fear that he would not lay on her mind heavily as she went to the kitchen for a bracing cup of coffee. She found her mother there watering the plants that lined the kitchen windowsill. There was no sign of her father anywhere. Emulating the breathless, happy tone that had colored her sister's voice for weeks before her wedding, Jen sang, "Good morning, Mom, where's Daddy?"

"He went to the hardware store," Ella answered placidly. "They're having a sale on electric hedge clippers."

"Did you tell him?" Jen asked tersely.

"No." Her watering finished, Ella turned to smile at her. "It's your bomb; I'll let you drop it." After replacing the long-spouted watering can in the cabinet beneath the sink, she frowned at the cup in Jen's hand. "Is that all you're having?"

"Are there any English muffins?" Jen asked, hoping there weren't.

There were, and Jen was determinedly chewing away when her father came whistling through the back door, a long package under one arm.

"Good morning, honey," he greeted her cheerfully. "Did you have a good time last night?"

Taking his question as her cue, Ella breezed out of the

159

kitchen after bestowing an encouraging smile on her daughter.

Catching his wife's parting look, and not being in the least obtuse, Ralph leveled his eyes on Jen and prompted, "What's up?"

"I'm getting married." Jen bit her lip hard the minute the last word was out of her mouth. Calling herself a blithering nitwit, she watched her father anxiously for a reaction. When it came it left her as stunned as her mother's had.

"Anyone I know?" Ralph asked blandly.

Jen should have realized his tone was just a little too bland, even coming from her even-tempered father. But in her surprise she didn't realize it, and his second question hit her like a shock of cold water.

"I want some answers, young lady," he barked angrily. "Who the hell is he?"

His face set, his eyes hard, he listened as Jen repeated, almost word for word, what she'd said to her mother only hours before. In a desperate bid to wipe the rigidity from his face, she finished on a soft, appealing whisper.

"I love him, Daddy."

Being a realistic man and loving his daughter very much, Ralph bowed to the inevitable.

"Okay, honey," he sighed. "When are we going to meet him?"

When, after exchanging hugs, kisses, and a few errant tears, Jen escaped to her room, it was with the conviction that if Adam failed to call she would leave home rather than try to explain.

The phone rang at exactly one minute after one.

CHAPTER 10

Adam presented himself at the Lengle residence at exactly six thirty, having arranged—with Jen acting as go-between—to take her parents out to dinner. His appearance when Jen opened the door was a small assault on nerves that were already drawn too tautly.

Although up until now his clothes had been obviously expensive, they had been casual sport clothes. Now, the sight of him in a fashionably cut suit, silk shirt and tie, and a fur-collared topcoat was just about enough to do her in entirely. Her reaction did not go unnoticed by Adam, although he did misinterpret it. Shrugging out of the topcoat as he stepped inside, he smiled wryly.

"It seems February is going to be every bit as bleak as January was. It is cold and it is windy."

In the process of handing his coat to her, the sleeves of both his suit and shirt inched up his arm, and Jen's glance was caught and held on the fine gold chain that encircled his narrow left wrist just below a slim gold watch.

"May I have it back?" Jen inquired huskily, knowing full well she did not have to identify "it."

"No," Adam answered flatly and, in an obvious attempt to change the subject, asked, "Where are your parents?"

"They'll be out in a minute." Glad for an excuse to avoid his eyes, Jen turned to drape his coat over the back of a chair. "They are being tactful by giving us some time alone together."

"That's very thoughtful of them."

161

Jen shuddered. She had not heard him move, yet he was right behind her—not touching, but very close. The shudder increased when he turned her to face him.

"You look like you're ready to fall apart," he said softly. "Was it very bad?" He knew she had told her parents about their plans to marry. But that was all he knew, for all she'd said over the phone was, "I talked to my mother and father." When she didn't answer at once he insisted, "Jennifer, are they angry?—disappointed?—what?"

"No," Jen denied. "At least, not any more. There were a few uncomfortable moments, but, well, I think they're reserving judgment until they've had a chance to get to know you."

"A commendable trait, reserving judgment until you have a base from which you can render a *fair* judgment." Adam smiled sardonically. "One their daughter should have cultivated."

Was he going to start that again? Jen went stiff with swift anger that, while churning her emotions, clouded her common sense. Shrugging off the hands that still clasped her shoulders, Jen lashed out at him unthinkingly.

"Yes, I know—I am childish, stupid, narrow-minded, straitlaced, morally uptight, and"—she tossed her head back defiantly, setting her red curls to dancing like flames around a log—"worst defect of all—I make snap judgments." Suddenly aware that her voice was rising, she drew a deep breath.

"Jen—" Adam began.

"One might wonder," she went on as if he hadn't spoken, "exactly what it is you see in me." Jen glared at him silently, challenging him to answer. He met the challenge in a way that drained the color from her face.

"You're fantastic in bed."

Her parents' entrance into the living room prevented her imminent explosion. Gritting her teeth and forcing a smile, she managed to get through the introductions and the flurry of activity of donning coats and getting into the car.

By the time they were seated in the tastefully decorated restaurant Adam had chosen, Jen had her seething emotions enough under control to look at Adam without fighting the urge to hiss like a ruffled cat.

Adam's behavior was faultless. As they made their leisurely way through an excellently prepared dinner Jen barely tasted, he responded to her parents' sometimes probing questions with a charmingly open earnestness that had them smiling contentedly into their after-dinner coffee.

During the drive back to the house the final straw fell on Jen's delicate emotional state when her father invited Adam to play golf with him. Her father *never* invited anyone to play golf until he knew them inside out! Even her sister's husband, Ron, had not been invited to play until a few weeks before they'd gotten married, and Ron had practically been a fixture around the house for months by that time!

Back at the house, feeling as battered as an overworked tennis ball, Jen gave up all hope of retaliation against Adam that night. After being told to make himself comfortable by her mother and being given a drink by her father, Adam sat, his teasing eyes taunting her, happily joining in as her parents made wedding plans.

That evening set the pattern for the weeks that followed. When, on the following afternoon, Jen had finally gotten him alone long enough to attack him for what he'd said, he'd replied, unanswerably, "Why not say it, darling? You *are* fantastic in bed." Then with a grimace he'd launched his own attack. "And if I somehow manage to live through the next four months, I'm hoping the reward will be worth all the effort."

Jen would have dearly loved to argue with him. The only problem was, she wasn't quite sure she fully understood what he was talking about. And before she could

163

marshal her thoughts, he had further confounded her by presenting her with a perfectly beautiful solitaire diamond set into an intricately wrought ring.

In the weeks that followed, Jen found they had more in common than a mutual physical attraction. She loved his town house on sight which, he admitted at once, was a relief to him as he loved it himself. Their preferences in furniture ran on parallel lines. Their taste in music was complementary, and they enjoyed the same sports. They had already discovered they liked the same foods while at the motel. Now Jen learned that liking extended to nearly everything edible down to the dark sweet chocolate that covered their favorite caramels.

The most delightful discovery came one night while they watched TV when her parents were out for an evening of cards at the home of friends. After roaring together at the offbeat sense of humor of a British comedy show, they had gone to the kitchen to raid the refrigerator for a snack. They reentered the living room just as the title of the late-night movie flashed onto the screen. The film was a classic from the forties and one of Jen's favorites. Studying her rapt expression as she read every one of the credits, Adam asked, "Do you want to watch it?"

"Would you mind?" Jen glanced at him quickly.

"Not at all," he grinned. "As a matter of fact, I love these old tear-jerkers."

Up until that point Jen had kept Adam at arm's length as far as physical contact was concerned. And much to her surprise, he had shown remarkable patience. Not once had he even tried to deepen their usual passionless good-night kiss. But she was weakening. She had started out loving him, and as the weeks blended into months and their compatability wove silken, enclosing threads over and around her senses, she discovered her love growing into frightening proportions. And undermining her determination to stick to her vow, she was gradually losing her fear of the future.

164

When the movie started they were seated over a foot apart on the sofa. By the time it came to a heart-wrenching end, Jen was wrapped in Adam's arms. The transition of being held close while sitting up, to being held closer while lying flat, was completed during the length of one mutually hungry kiss.

Partial sanity returned to Jen when Adam's trembling fingers began unbuttoning her shirt-style blouse. When the tips of his fingers brushed the exposed skin at the edge of her bra, she murmured an unconvincing protest.

"Oh, God, Jennifer," Adam groaned raggedly. "Being away from you again for two weeks is going to be hard enough as it is. Let me love you before I go, darling."

"Go!" Jen went stiff with shock. "Where are you going now?"

During the last months Adam had had to leave the country four times, and Jen had writhed with an uncertainty she couldn't control on each occasion. To add to her uneasiness he had looked more harried and tired after each successive trip. And although her mind was filled with a riot of questions about his activities while he was away, she bit them back, sure he would resent them. The fact that he became cold and withdrawn for several days following his return each time was an added barrier to any open discussion. After his last trip, two weeks previously, he had told her he most probably would not have to go away again before the wedding. In her overwhelming relief, Jen had conveniently forgotten his cautionary "most probably."

Now she added dully, "When?"

"I told you I might have to leave the country once more before June," Adam rasped. "I fly out tomorrow morning."

"You were going without telling me!"

"Of course not," he snapped. Swinging his legs to the floor, he stood up. "But being fairly sure of your reaction

165

to my going, I decided to wait until the last minute to tell you."

Hating herself yet unable to keep the accusation from pouring from her mouth Jen cried, "And was that last-minute telling to come by way of a note claiming you had an emergency call?"

The moment the words were out Jen wished them back. Not once during the preceding months had she questioned him as to why he'd had to leave the motel so precipitously that morning—simply because it hadn't mattered. He *had* called her. He *had* asked her to marry him. And as far as she was concerned, she had enough doubts in the present, worrying about the future, not to rake up the past. Why, she asked herself, had she brought it up now? Apparently he was asking the same question.

"Dammit, Jennifer, you—" Adam broke off to give her a hard stare, then, turning away abruptly, he ground out, "Oh, the hell with it." Striding across the room, he scooped up his jacket, growled "Good night," and without looking back, slammed out of the house.

Time after time during the weeks that followed Adam's departure Jen berated herself for her foolish tongue. But always on the next thought she berated Adam for springing his news on her the way he had. And just when she was beginning to feel easy with him. His reaction to her charge, his abrupt departure, all seemed a little too suspicious to her. Mistrust of the necessity for his going reared its ugly head. The fact that she heard nothing from him did nothing to allay that mistrust.

Luckily her parents accepted Adam's absence with complacency, their attitude being, a man had a job to do and he did it.

As the wedding arrangements jelled and came together, Jen threw herself into the last-minute craziness with a frenzy that was mistaken for excitement. As the stated two weeks came and then passed, Jen felt she could show real excitement if she could be positive the bridegroom would show up.

In the short amount of time allotted, Ella Lengle had outdone herself. Two weeks to the day of being told her daughter was getting married she had hired the caterer and ordered the invitations.

The wedding and reception would be held in the large backyard, the food set out buffet style in the cool garage, along with a makeshift bar. Jen's only attendant would be her sister. Adam's best man was to be a close friend from his college days who Jen had met once. Ella's only fears were that the rose bushes would not bloom in time—and that it would rain.

Sixteen days from the day he left, Adam returned. Jen had had no word of any kind, and when the doorbell rang she ran to answer it, hoping against hope. When she opened the door there he stood, looking tired and a little drawn, a sardonic smile curving his lips.

"Where you afraid—or hoping—my plane had gone down over the Pacific?" he drawled.

The atmosphere between them was decidedly cool for several days.

Her mother had promptly invited him to dinner, and over their after-dinner coffee Adam said smoothly, "Oh, by the way, darling, I saw mother while I was away, and she sends you her love, her regrets, and her promise of a fabulous wedding gift as soon as she gets back to the States."

Adam had informed them that first night that none of his family could make the wedding as they were all out of the country. At Jen's raised eyebrows and look of surprise, he'd explained that his mother was overseas on an extended leave of absence. He had then explained to her parents that his father and brother were permanent residents of Japan.

The ruffled waters between Adam and Jen smoothed

out enough so that by rehearsal time—the night before the wedding—they were even smiling at each other again.

Jen's wedding day dawned pink and beautiful, and by the time Jen's brother-in-law placed the stereo arm on "Here Comes the Bride," the sky was a sunshine-spattered, cloud-free blue.

Everything was perfect and went off like clockwork. The ceremony at eleven. The allotted thirty minutes for picture taking directly after the knot was tied. The announcement of luncheon being served at eleven forty-five, thereby allowing two hours and forty-five minutes for Jen and Adam to be duly toasted, have some lunch, cut the cake, and circulate among their guests before slipping inside to change and leave in time to make their plane, destination unknown to all but Adam and Jen.

Following the game plan like a well-trained soldier, Jen looked around for Adam at two twenty-five. When he was obviously not in the crush in the yard or at the bar, she headed for the house. On opening the screen door to go in she encountered Vicki on her way out.

"If you're looking for Adam," Vicki said in an oddly strained tone, "he's in Daddy's den. He has a visitor, and when he asked me if there was somewhere they could talk privately, I told him to go in there."

"Thanks, Vic."

As she walked by Vicki, Jen gave a fleeting thought to her strange tone, but in too much of a hurry to linger and ask about it, she shrugged it off and headed for the den. The door was slightly ajar, and with a gentle push Jen opened it a few inches more, a smile and words of apology on her lips. The words were never uttered and the smile faded from her lips as Jen stood transfixed, staring at her husband of two and a half hours and the exquisitely lovely, sobbing woman he held so protectively in his arms.

The woman was obviously Oriental, or at least partly so. Tiny in comparison to Adam, she had long, straight, shiny, raven-black hair and a face that belonged on a delicate silk wall hanging. And at the moment her dark, almond-shaped eyes looked heart-catchingly beautiful drenched in tears. Jen took one unsteady step back, then froze as the woman's soft lilting voice came faintly to her.

"I-do-not-wish-to-sound-ungrateful-Adam-but-I-don't--know-how-I-can-bear-it."

Jen bit down hard on her lip as Adam's hand came up to stroke the silky black hair. Her teeth dug in harder when the afternoon sunlight struck glintingly off the fine gold chain looped around his wrist. The softly soothing sound of Adam's reply drove her back another step.

"The pain will ease, eventually, I promise you. And if you ever need me, I'll be there, always."

Numb, Jen was unaware of her bridal bouquet sliding out of her frozen fingers. Turning slowly, she walked blindly down the hall and into her bedroom. Standing at the foot of her bed, staring at nothing, her hands smoothed the material at the front of her gown over and over again. She was still standing there, smoothing, when Adam entered the room some ten minutes later.

"Jennifer."

The sound of his voice reached her; the tone of sharp concern did not. Blinking her eyes, she focused on him and saw the small bouquet he held in one hand.

"We have to change and get out of here or we'll miss our plane." Adam spoke slowly, carefully. "And you have to toss this"—he lifted her flowers—"to the single girls."

"Yes, of course." Her movements jerky, Jen turned away from him, her hands going to the zipper at the back of her neck. Then, except for the slight trembling in her fingers, she became still again. Her voice sounded gratingly harsh in the quiet room. "Has she gone?"

"Jennifer—"

"Has she gone?"

"Yes." Adam sighed wearily. "She had asked the cabbie to wait." He sighed again, this time from right behind her. "Jennifer, she didn't—"

"I think you said something about having to change," Jen interrupted sharply, her fingers tugging at the zipper. The bouquet flew by her, landing on the bed. Jen went stiff as his fingers brushed hers.

"Let me do that," he growled. Jen stood as lifeless as a mannequin until the zipper reached the end of its track, then she moved away from him with a terse "Thank you."

Somehow she got through it. Changing clothes in the same room with him. Tossing her flowers to the laughing group of single girls and managing a teasing remark when Liz, blushing bright pink, caught it. Responding to the hugs, kisses and the good wishes of everyone. Smiling all the while. Somehow she got through it all.

Inside the car the atmosphere was electric with a tense silence. Unable to bare her highly imaginative thoughts, Jen launched into nonsensical chatter.

"Did you see the look that passed between Liz and Ted when she caught the bouquet?" Jen despaired at the false lightness of her trite tone, yet unable to face the strained silence, she went on, "I don't think it will be too long before they're facing a minister—"

"Shut up, Jennifer."

Her breath failed her as Adam's voice slashed across her jabbering. The very roughness of his tone produced the quiet he obviously wanted, for hurt by the harsh order, Jen withdrew, firmly hanging on to thoughts of Liz and Ted.

How perfectly suited to each other they seemed to be, she thought enviously. Liz had been the first person Jen had called about her and Adam's engagement.

"I knew he wasn't the one-night-stand type," Liz had exclaimed gleefully. "I can't wait to tell Ted. When can we get together, Jen?"

Although Jen had winced at the way Liz had phrased her opening statement, she had laughed and promised to get back to her about a dinner date for the four of them.

They had spent several evenings together during the last

170

months and the camaraderie they had shared at the motel had been solidly reestablished.

Jen had no idea how long they'd been driving before she realized they were not heading for the airport, or that Adam had not said a word since demanding she shut up. Although she was sure she knew the answer, she asked, "Where are we going?"

"Home." Adam's tight lips hardly moved around the one word.

"But we'll miss our plane!" Shifting around, Jen looked directly at him, then wished she hadn't. His mouth twisted derisively, and the glance he shot her held cool contempt. He didn't bother to reply but returned his concentration to the road.

Jen didn't attempt to break the silence for the remainder of the ride to the house. Hands clenched in her lap, she nurtured her anger while trying to ignore the feeling of loss his glance had instilled.

When they reached the house she preceded him inside with a cool detachment she was nowhere near feeling. Inside she was a churning mass of emotions and urges, the uppermost being the urge to fling accusations at him. The only thing that kept her silent was the childish determination that he speak first.

Walking into the large rectangular living room, she stopped in the middle of the floor, back to him, and waited.

Still without a word to her, she heard him walk across the room and then the dull rattle of plastic against plastic as he lifted the mouthpiece to the phone and punched out a number. In disbelief she heard him cancel their flight reservations and then punch out another number. Unable to contain herself she spun around to face him as he coolly canceled their hotel reservations in Hawaii. With a sigh of regret, she said good-bye to all the secret hopes she'd had for their time together at that hotel.

Adam's face was expressionless when, his phone call

finished, he looked at her. "So much for that bright idea." He smiled wryly. "I don't think either of us are in the mood for the honeymoon suite now." One dark eyebrow lifted questioningly. "Are you ready to hear it?"

"No!" Spinning around, Jen walked jerkily across the room, lengthening the distance between them. In her blind haste to get away from him, and in her fear of hearing him tell her the tiny beauty he'd been holding was a "friend," she scraped her leg on the corner of an occasional table as she hurried by.

"Jennifer!" Adam's warning, coming an instant too late, followed her sharp gasp of pain. With a few long strides he was by her side, his hands grasping her upper arms to steady her. "How long is it going to take you to realize what a foolish young woman you are?" His harsh tone was emphasized by a lightly administered shake.

"Adam, I don't—" What she'd wanted to tell him was she didn't have the sophistication to live the way his parents did. That she was selfish, and possessive, and the idea of sharing him with someone else was unendurable. He didn't give her the chance to say it.

"Yeah, I know," he cut in bitterly. "You don't want to hear it." He gave her that oddly sad smile. "I thought I heard the gavel drop when I picked your flowers up off the hall floor."

"What?" Jen stared at him in confusion.

"You had made your judgment then already, hadn't you?" Adam rasped. "And the verdict was: Adam Banner, guilty as charged."

"Adam, stop—" Jen began, and again he cut in fiercely.

"Stop what?" Suddenly all the harshness was gone, in his hands as well as his voice. "Stop hoping, praying, that you'll begin to see sense?" His hands moved up her arms and over her shoulders caressingly. "Stop aching for the woman I know you can be?" Bending his head, he brushed his lips along the taut line of her jaw to her ear. "Jennifer —Jennifer," he murmured. "This is our wedding day. You are my wife. I don't want to fight with you." His lips moved seductively to the corner of her trembling mouth. "I want to love with you." Sliding his mouth over her slightly parted lips, he whispered, "And I know you want it too."

Jen's resistance was very short-lived simply because, with his mouth moving in drugging enticement on hers and his hands evoking a trembling response from her body, she didn't want to resist. Sighing softly, she left her forgotten handbag drop to the floor and, slipping her arms around his neck, parted her lips still further for him.

Adam gave a muffled groan and, sweeping her up into his arms, mounted the open, spiral staircase to the second floor and their bedroom.

Slowly, taking time to stroke, caress, explore, they undressed each other until her only adornments were her wedding band and the engagement ring that complemented it, and his, a larger matching band that circled his finger and a fine gold chain that circled his wrist.

When, finally, he stretched his length beside her on the cool sheets, she lifted her mouth to his, eagerly, breathlessly.

"I was beginning to be afraid our interrupted journey was never going to be resumed," Adam groaned against Jen's hungry lips. The quivering response that sent the heat pounding through the pliant body she arched against him seemed to rob him of all control. His voice a hoarse incitement, he warned, "I don't know how much longer I can wait, darling. It's been so long and I want you so badly."

They spent their honeymoon week in seclusion in the house, the majority of the time in the bedroom. As if by mutual agreement the subject of the exquisite, dark-haired woman was studiously avoided. With an iron determination Jen had not realized she was capable of, she pushed all thoughts and fears of the future to the deepest reaches of her mind.

In the weeks that followed, their life fell into a pattern that Jen kept pleasant by simply refusing to acknowledge, let alone face, the uncertainty that hovered at the fringes of her consciousness.

Adam was kept busy and worked long hours settling into the executive position he'd been given by his company. Jen kept herself busy after working hours by playing housewife. That there seemed to be a hush-before-the-storm, waiting atmosphere surrounding them, she ignored with an unfamiliar adroitness.

As the days grew long and hot with summer, Jen allowed herself the luxury of believing the growing closeness between them could cancel the necessity of an eventual confrontation. Her cocoon of complacency was shattered in mid-July, six weeks to the day of their wedding.

In an effort to more quickly familiarize himself with the routine of his newly acquired department, Adam had worked most Saturday mornings. On this fateful morning Jen was dawdling over her second cup of coffee while glancing over the morning paper when the phone rang.

After a coolly impersonal "Hello" Jen's voice took on a sincere warmth on finding her caller was Liz. Although she and Adam had been out to dinner with Liz and Ted twice since their marriage, it had been over a week since Jen had heard from Liz. Jen soon learned the purpose of Liz's call was both urgent and exciting.

"Jen, please, *please* say you can go shopping with me this morning," Liz pleaded exaggeratedly.

"Okay," Jen laughed. "I can go shopping with you this morning. Now, do you think you could tell me why you sound like you're ready to explode?"

"We're getting married," Liz laughed. "Ted and I, I mean." Before Jen could get a word of surprise or congratulations in, Liz bubbled on, "He's been at me about it for weeks and last night, in a weak moment, I said yes. Jen, honey, you would not believe this man. When he decides to do something he doesn't horse around. He's picking me up late this afternoon, and we're taking an early-evening flight to Vegas. Vegas! Do you believe it?" Liz paused to gasp at a quick breath, then plunged on, "And I am determined to be completely outfitted. Can you be ready in a half hour? I'll pick you up, and we'll go into Philly to the Gallery."

It was not until after she was settled into the passenger seat of Liz's car that Jen remembered she had not called Adam. *Oh, well,* she smiled to herself, *it will be more fun to tell him in person anyway.*

It was after three when Liz stopped the car in front of the town house. Jen felt as if she'd been in a marathon race as they had dashed in and out of the many shops in the tiered shopping mall, pausing only long enough to gulp a quick lunch of sandwiches and iced tea.

"Oh, God, I've got to run or I'll never be ready when Ted arrives," Liz chattered, leaning over to give Jen a quick hug. "Thanks for going with me. Give Adam my love, and tell him we'll call when we get back."

Jen was smiling in anticipation of Adam's reaction to her news when she walked into the living room. The sight of Adam, still dressed in the lightweight business suit he'd put on that morning, a suitcase on the floor beside him, standing tense and tight-faced by the phone, wiped the smile from her lips.

"Where the hell have you been?" His harshly impatient tone brought her to an abrupt halt. "I've been calling everyone I could think of trying to find you. It's too late now, I've got to go." Shooting his left sleeve, he glanced at his watch and shook his head sharply before bending to grab the handle of his valise.

"Go? It's too late?" Jen repeated in shocked confusion. "Adam, what are you talking about?"

"Jennifer, I've got to go," Adam said gently. "The executive jet's waiting for me."

Anger spurred by renewed fear made Jen go hot, then cold. Where was this jet waiting to take him? Where or—

175

the insidious thought crept into her mind—to whom? Watching him walk toward her, Jen was suddenly terrified by the thought that if he left now, their relationship would be irreparably damaged.

When he bent to kiss her she stepped back, twisting her head aside. "I thought you were finished with the traveling part of the business," she accused.

"This is different," Adam sighed, raking his hand through his hair. "There is no time to explain now. I have no choice, I must go."

The four words *I have no choice* hit Jen almost like a physical blow. Her reaction to the pain and fear gripping her was totally human, and completely contradictory. Her tone thick with sarcasm, she snapped, "Another *emergency* call, Adam?"

Adam's body stiffened, then, turning away from her, he walked to the door. "As a matter of fact, it was." He turned the knob and opened the door before adding, "Only *this* time my father's *dying.*" Without a backward glance he walked out of the house.

Jen never knew how long she stood staring at the door, her eyes wide with shock and horror. Adam's father was dying, and she had sent him away in anger. The shudder that tore through her body broke the self-condemning trance that held her motionless. What had she done?

Adam was away for ten days. Ten long days during which Jen examined his parting shot, "Only *this* time my father's *dying.*" Oh, the remark itself was fairly obvious. With those six terse words he'd told her clearly that his sudden departure from the motel had been due to his father's health. No, it wasn't his statement she didn't understand, it was his tone that nagged at her. What, exactly, had that tone conveyed? Sadness surely, but there was something else. Exasperation? Anger? Defeat? She couldn't pinpoint it, and so it tormented her.

Feeling suddenly very young and not too bright, Jen

176

lived through those ten days by telling herself Adam *would* come back.

She was sitting on the sofa, staring sightlessly at the news on TV, when he came home after ten days of total silence. Without speaking, he dropped his suitcase to the floor inside the door, crossed the room, and sighing wearily, sank onto the end of the sofa, stretching his legs out with another long sigh.

Jen's heart contracted painfully at the look of him. His face was pale, with lines of strain etched deeply around his mouth, and he looked exhausted. Her voice husky with compassion Jen whispered, "Your father?"

"He's gone," Adam said quietly, his eyes studying the tips of his shoes.

"I'm sorry, Adam." Jen choked around the tears clogging her throat. "I'm—I'm sorry for everything."

"What does 'everything' mean?" Adam raised bleak eyes to hers. "Sorry you ever laid eyes on me? Sorry you married me?"

"Adam!" Jen exclaimed, shocked at the utter defeat in his tone. "You can't believe that?"

"I don't know what I believe anymore, Jennifer." Getting to his feet he stared broodingly at her a moment, then, swinging away, he walked out of the room with a muttered "And I'm too beat to go into it now. Good night, Jennifer."

Good night! Good night? Stunned, Jen sat staring at the empty doorway. *No!* Anger ignited by fear catapulted her to her feet. *Dammit, no!* Tired or not, he could not let her hang like this. She would not let him. There had been too many things left unsaid. There were explanations to be given—by both of them. And the time was now. Scared but determined she walked to the stairs.

Expecting to find Adam in bed, Jen was surprised to see him standing by the window, his hands thrust into his pants pockets. He had removed his jacket and tie, and had opened the buttons on his short-sleeved shirt. He didn't turn around when she entered the room, yet she knew he was aware of her presence.

"Adam?"

"What?"

He didn't turn around, and the flat, indifferent tone of his voice sent a shaft of unease through her.

"Why"—Jen wet her dry lips—"why didn't you tell me your father was ill?"

"Why?" Now he turned, and Jen almost wished he hadn't. His expression held both anger and disbelief. "Why?" He repeated mockingly. "Because you were so obviously uninterested, that's why."

"B-but I—I," Jen sputtered, unable to believe she'd heard him right. Had he really accused her of being uninterested?

"But hell," he spat savagely across her stuttering words. "You've made it very clear—from the beginning—what you wanted from this marriage, and interest in my father, or any other area of my life, wasn't part of it."

"What are you talking about?" Jen gasped.

"You know damned well what I'm talking about," he snarled. "Why did you leave my bed that morning?" he demanded.

"Be-because—I—I" Jen floundered at the suddenness of his question, her cheeks flushing pink.

"Because you were ashamed of what had happened there," Adam said flatly.

"No, Adam!" Jen protested. "I—"

"I needed you that morning," Adam's thickened voice cut through her protest. "My mother was damn near hysterical when she called me. She pleaded with me to come at once. You see, the doctors had told my brother they didn't know if he'd live until we could get there." His tone went rough. "I had to go, and I needed to see you, and you weren't there."

"But when you came back, Adam, you never said anything," Jen cried.

"I *did* try. You said it wasn't important." His lips twisted unpleasantly. "It didn't take long to figure what *was* important to you."

"What do you mean?" By the tone of his voice Jen was sure she would not like his answer. She was right.

"That bed." Adam jerked his head at their bed. "I should have kept my hands off you. I should have left you unawakened and safe in your tight, moralistic world. You couldn't face it, could you? So in your shame you went sneaking away. And when I got back and called you, needing you even more, you were prepared to cut me dead, weren't you?"

"Adam, no! You don't understand. I was—" Jen got no further.

"You were hungry." He flung the accusation at her. "You have a hungry body and a greedy mouth, both of which very obviously drive me crazy. And when I asked you to marry me you said yes simply to make that hunger legal and moral. *That's* what's important to you."

"That is not true, Adam," Jen denied fiercely.

"No?" Adam's brows arched exaggeratedly. "Then why have you never asked any questions, not even about the woman who came to your parents' home the day of the wedding?"

"Because I was afraid," Jen shouted at him, goaded beyond endurance.

"Afraid of what, for God's sake?" he shouted back.

"Of losing you. Of boring you. Of not being able to hold your interest," Jen sobbed, brushing at the tears that were suddenly running down her face. "After the way you grew up, and the life-style you were used to"—she waved her hand in self-dismissal—"what could I possibly offer you?"

"Jennifer!"

"No, let me finish," Jen insisted. "Can you try and imagine how—how dull my life suddenly seemed while I was listening to you tell me about yours? Can you try and imagine how bland and uninteresting I felt? When I read your note the first thing I thought was that having had your fun, you had decided to skip the good-byes—and possible recriminations."

"Dammit, Jennifer," Adam began angrily, but Jen went on doggedly.

"But—well—remembering how we'd been together, I—I just knew you were not like that."

"Thanks for that, anyway," Adam inserted wryly.

"Adam, please," Jen cried. "It was during the week you were away that I convinced myself that even if you did call or come to me, I couldn't possibly hold you. That's why I said it didn't matter. If you had let it go at that I would have gotten over you—eventually." She shook her head. "But once I saw you again, and you held me in your arms, and kissed me, I—I. . . . What you said is true, Adam; I am hungry. But only for you." Her voice dropped to a whispered sob. "Only for you. And I've felt like I've been walking a tightrope all these weeks. I've been so afraid you'd come and tell me it was over, or that you wouldn't come at all. For you see, Adam, I thought that the physical thing was all we had going."

"Oh, God, angel!" Adam was across the room in a few long strides and pulling her into his arms. "I know I'm a little defensive about my parents, but I never dreamed I was giving you the impression I wanted to live like that. I don't." Lifting his hand, he wiped away the tears still trickling down her face. "I never did. And I'd grown tired of the traveling over a year ago. I even considered taking one of the desk jobs offered to me. The hang-up was, every time I came home this house seemed so damned empty, and I never met a woman that stirred enough interest in me to even consider the idea of installing her here." Suddenly his eyes darkened to that bone-melting look of warm velvet. "That is until I walked into that bar at the motel. You stirred all kinds of interest. The day I left the motel I told my mother I was going to marry you."

"She's been in Japan this whole time, hasn't she?" Jen asked softly.

"Yes," Adam sighed. "She's still there. She'll stay until all the legalities are straightened out. She can't wait to meet you. She told me no woman can be as perfect or beautiful as I've described you to be." Adam grinned.

"Oh, Adam." Jen stared up at him, her legs going weak at the expression of love on his face. "I love you so very much."

"And I love you." Sliding his fingers into her hair, he bent his head and brushed her mouth with his lips. "Why are we standing here talking?" He murmured huskily.

"Oh, Adam, I'm sorry," Jen cried contritely. "You must be exhausted."

"I'm tired, yes," he agreed softly. "But that isn't what I meant. I've been away ten days, and to a man in love who is as hungry for his wife as I am for you, ten days can seem as long as ten months."

It was later, as she lay replete and relaxed beside him, murmuring contentedly as Adam continued to stroke her skin as if he couldn't get enough of the feel of her, that Jen was struck by a sudden thought. Giving him a gentle push, she sat up and tried, unsuccessfully, to glare at him.

"Who was that woman, Adam?" she demanded softly.

Adam's soft laughter tickled her spine, and she couldn't even make a pretense of resistance when he drew her back down beside him.

"My father's 'friend.'" Adam's warm breath disturbed a few tendrils at her temple; it disturbed her pulse rate as well. "I had told you at the motel that she was an exquisite woman. She took his illness very badly. I pulled a few strings and got her a job in Dallas. She was on her way there, between planes, when she came to your parents' house." While he was speaking, his breath teased in a dancing, erratic line to the corner of her mouth. Jen's pulses seemed about to jump out of her body when the tip of his tongue began an exploration of that corner. "Any more questions?"

"One," Jen gasped.

"Mmmmm?"

"Aren't you ever going to kiss me?"

Jen waked to an empty bed and a silent house. Sitting up, she strained her ears to catch the slightest noise. "Adam?" *Strange,* she mused when there was no answer to her call. Adam had long since ceased going to his office on Saturday mornings. *Very strange. Is the honeymoon over?* she asked herself humorously.

All traces of humor had fled by the time she'd finished glancing over the morning paper, had consumed a glass of juice, two pieces of thin wheat toast, and two cups of coffee. Where the devil was he?

After making the bed she dressed in jeans, an old sweatshirt, and—remembering the full waste can in the kitchen and the snow on the ground—low boots, then went back to the kitchen to wash up her breakfast dishes.

As she wiped the butcherblock table, Jen fought the images that flashed in and out of her mind. Images of icy roads and sliding tires and the carnage of wrecked cars and bodies.

She had been so ecstatically, unbelievably happy the last six months that sometimes it almost scared her. And although she wouldn't admit it even to herself, she was scared now. Pushing the growing feeling of unease to the very fringes of her mind, she hummed snatches of a popular song while shooting anxious glances at the clock. She was wringing her dishcloth over the sink when she heard the front door open and Adam call, "Jennifer?"

Fingers clutching spasmodically at the dishcloth, Jen slumped against the sink, weak from the rush of relief that washed over her. In the few seconds it took him to reach the kitchen she had control of herself.

"Where in the world have you—"

"Put your jacket on and come with me," Adam ordered, interrupting her. "I want to show you something."

"Adam, what—" Jen's voice trailed off, for after walking out of the kitchen, Adam went to the hall closet.

"Adam!"

"Come on," he urged, holding her jacket for her. "You'd better wear your cap and gloves too. It's cold outside."

Momentarily giving up the battle, Jen put on her jacket and, cap and gloves in hand, followed him to the car, glancing around to admire the sun-sparkling whiteness of the four inches of snow that covered the front lawn. As soon as the car was in motion she tried again.

"Adam, where did you go this morning?"

"To look at a car," Adam flashed her a grin. "I woke up early and saw it advertised for sale as I skimmed the paper. I didn't have the heart to wake you, so I decided to run look at it myself and bring some Danish for breakfast on the way back."

"So, where's the Danish?"

"Oh—I forgot it," Adam answered vaguely.

"And now you're taking me to see the car?"

"No, I bought it." His grin flashed again. "For you. It's an early Valentine gift."

"A Valentine gift?" Jen exclaimed incredulously. "A car? Adam, are you crazy?"

"Sure," he answered complacently. "About you."

"Okay." Jen sighed. "I give up. Are you going to tell me where we're going?" He had made several turns, and now they were out of the more populated area on a back road where the homes were set much farther apart.

"I told you," Adam replied. "I want to show you something. I had to drive back this way to look at the car, and that's when I saw it." He paused, then smiled. "Ah, there it is."

They were approaching a bend in the road, and just before they reached it Adam drove the car off the macadam onto a flat, snow-covered verge about six feet wide. They parked at the base of a rather steep incline at the top of which was a high chain link fence. Looking around in confusion, Jen said, "I don't see anything."

"Not here," Adam laughed. "We have to get out of the car. Come on."

After pulling her cap onto her head and tugging her gloves over her hands, Jen scrambled out of the car and through the snow to where Adam waited for her, hand outstretched. Grasping her hand, he strode off around the bend in the road at the foot of the incline, which became lower and lower as they walked. Where Adam came to a stop the incline had dropped to a low bank and Jen could see the chain link fence surrounded a tot-lot, closed now for the winter.

"There," Adam nodded at the tot-lot. "That's what I wanted you to see."

"A tot-lot?" Jen exclaimed.

"No, the bank, Jennifer," Adam said softly. "A perfect place for angels in the snow."

"Angels in the—" Jen began in astonishment, and then she grew silent as the significance of his carefully spoken words hit her. They were the exact words she'd said to him exactly one year ago. "Oh, Adam." She choked around the emotion clogging her throat. Spinning around, she gazed up at him and felt her throat close altogether at the tender expression on his face.

"Come on," he challenged softly when he saw her blink against the moisture clouding her eyes. "I bet I can make a better angel than you can."

Turning around, he flung himself backward onto the bank, long arms and legs flapping vigorously. Laughing like a ten-year-old, Jen ran several paces below him and dropped into the snow on the bank. She had just begun to flap her arms and legs when Adam sprang to his feet and came to stand beside her.

"Now you ruined the skirt," Jen scolded, holding her hand out for him to hoist her to her feet.

Ignoring her hand, Adam dropped to his knees. His warm velvet eyes caressing her face, he pulled off his gloves—exposing a fine gold chain coiled around his narrow wrist—and let them fall to the ground. Cradling her face in his hands, he lowered his head and kissed her gently.

"Who needs snow angels," Adam murmured as he lifted his head, "when they can have the real thing? You've made me very happy, Jennifer."

"I'm glad," Jen whispered huskily. "I love you very much, Adam."

"I know," Adam whispered back. "And the knowing fills everything inside of me to the point of bursting."

His mouth touched hers again, and with a groan Adam lowered his body and stretched his length on top of her. His lips grew hard with demand and, clasping his hands more tightly to her head, he kissed her with merciless passion until he heard her soft moan of surrender. Sliding his lips from hers, he teased, "Lift your head—I want to bite your neck."

The sound of a car driving by on the road brought Jen to her senses.

"Adam, stop," she gasped as his tongue went sliding down the side of her neck. "Anyone driving by can see us. What will people think?"

"That we are obviously in love and having a romp in the snow." Adam laughed, jumping to his feet. "And they'll envy us and wish they were so lucky."

Reaching down, he grasped Jen's hands and pulled her up in front of him.

"Come on, snow angel, let's go home," Adam grinned wickedly. "Those poor devils don't know the half of it."

"THE MOST
ROMANTIC
NOVEL
SINCE
LOVE
STORY"
—Good Housekeeping

Change of Heart

SALLY MANDEL

Once in a long while, a
story is so bursting with
tenderness that its charm
is irresistible.

That story is Sharlie and
Brian's story. *Change of Heart*—
a love story for a lifetime.

A Dell Book $2.95 (11355-5)

**VOLUME I
IN THE EPIC
NEW SERIES**

*The Morland
Dynasty*

The Founding

by Cynthia Harrod-Eagles

THE FOUNDING, a panoramic saga rich with passion and excitement, launches Dell's most ambitious series to date—THE MORLAND DYNASTY.

From the Wars of the Roses and Tudor England to World War II, THE MORLAND DYNASTY traces the lives, loves and fortunes of a great English family.

A DELL BOOK $3.50   #12677-0

Once you've tasted joy and passion, do you dare dream of

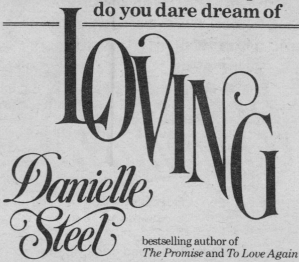

LOVING

Danielle Steel

bestselling author of
The Promise and *To Love Again*

Bettina Daniels lived in a gilded world—pampered, adored, adoring. She had youth, beauty and a glamorous life that circled the globe—everything her father's love, fame and money could buy. Suddenly, Justin Daniels was gone. Bettina stood alone before a mountain of debts and a world of strangers—men who promised her many things, who tempted her with words of love. But Bettina had to live her own life, seize her own dreams and take her own chances. But could she pay the bittersweet price?

A Dell Book ================================ $3.50 (14684-4)

She was born with a woman's passion, a warrior's destiny, and a beauty no man could resist.

Firebrand's Woman

Vanessa Royall

Author of *Wild Wind Westward* and
Come Faith, Come Fire

Gyva—a beautiful half-breed cruelly banished from her tribe, she lived as an exile in the white man's alien world.

Firebrand—the legendary Chickasaw chief, he swore to defend his people against the hungry settlers. He also swore to win back Gyva. Together in the face of defeat, they will forge a brave and victorious new dream.

A Dell Book   **$2.95   (12597-9)**

At your local bookstore or use this handy coupon for ordering:

The unforgettable saga of a magnificent family

IN JOY AND IN SORROW

by JOAN JOSEPH

They were the wealthiest Jewish family in Portugal, masters of Europe's largest shipping empire. Forced to flee the scourge of the Inquisition that reduced their proud heritage to ashes, they crossed the ocean in a perilous voyage. Led by a courageous, beautiful woman, they would defy fate to seize a forbidden dream of love.

A Dell Book   **$3.50**   **(14367-5)**